The game is *The Village of Fate.*

Even if it's just because of
some characters in a game,
I want to change.

I leaned back in my chair to stretch and looked over at the tank. My eyes met those of my resident escape artist, who was hanging halfway out of the top.

THE NPCs IN THIS VILLAGE SIM GAME MUST BE REAL! ↵

NOVEL

02

WRITTEN BY

Hirukuma

ILLUSTRATED BY

Namako

Seven Seas Entertainment

▶NPC Short for non-player character.
[NOUN] A character which the player cannot control.

CONTENTS

MURAZUKURI GAME NO NPC GA NAMAMI
NO NINGEN TOSHIKA OMOENAI Vol. 2
©Hirukuma 2020
First published in Japan in 2020 by
KADOKAWA CORPORATION, Tokyo.
English translation rights arranged with
KADOKAWA CORPORATION, Tokyo.

Seven Seas press and purchase enquiries can be sent to
Marketing Manager Lianne Sentar at press@gomanga.com.
Information regarding the distribution and purchase of
digital editions is available from Digital Manager CK Russell
at digital@gomanga.com.

Follow Seven Seas Entertainment online at
sevenseasentertainment.com.

TRANSLATION: Alexandra Owen-Burns
ADAPTATION: Aysha U. Farah
COVER DESIGN: Hanase Qi
LOGO DESIGN: George Panella
INTERIOR LAYOUT & DESIGN: Clay Gardner
COPY EDITOR: Jade Gardner
LIGHT NOVEL EDITOR: Rebecca Scoble
PREPRESS TECHNICIAN: Melanie Ujimori
PRINT MANAGER: Rhiannon Rasmussen-Silverstein
PRODUCTION MANAGER: Lissa Pattillo
MANAGING EDITOR: Julie Davis
ASSOCIATE PUBLISHER: Adam Arnold
PUBLISHER: Jason DeAngelis

ISBN: 978-1-64827-593-7
Printed in Canada
First Printing: January 2022
10 9 8 7 6 5 4 3 2 1

Prologue

THE WOMAN FIDDLED with her hair and stared at the brand-new PC monitor in front of her.

How interesting...

Yes, I like him. He's perfect.

I wonder how things will develop.

I wasn't inclined to think my judgment was wrong, but it would take time to be sure. I wanted to help him, but right now I could only watch.

I sighed, sitting back in my state-of-the-art leather chair.

"How boring."

Wait, what?

"I'm busy. Go do that over there."

What is it now? How annoying. I wanted to keep watching, but work was work. And all I could do right now was observe. How difficult.

"All right, all right! I know! Just wait a second! Don't touch this either! You'll mess it up!"

Good luck, Yoshio-kun. Remember that fate isn't always kind.

The voice called for the woman again. She sighed before slowly lifting herself out of her chair.

part 4

THE NEW VILLAGER ↵

THE NPCs IN THIS VILLAGE SIM GAME MUST BE REAL! ↵

chapter 01 The Villagers' Reunion and My Pride

"**T**HE BONUS EVENT starts now!"

This was what I'd been waiting for.

I had everything I needed on my desk: plenty of juice, several snacks, and some fruit from the Village of Fate. I figured I could eat my fruit at the same time my villagers ate theirs. I made sure to use the bathroom, too. I was ready to see this event through to the very end, regardless of length.

After the Day of Corruption, my villagers went out exploring. As a result, a much wider area of the map was visible to me now. I studied it intently, familiarizing myself with the layout before things kicked off.

In front of the cave was a fence made from logs, designed to stop monsters getting in. During the Day of Corruption, that fence played a huge role in keeping my villagers safe.

Just inside the fence stood a wooden watchtower, as well as a row of logs left out to dry. Eventually, I planned to use them to enclose some land for farming; there was already space cleared for it, just on the other side of the fence.

Luckily, there weren't many trees to start with; the people living here before gave us a head start. All that remained were a few stumps dotted around, giving my villagers a clear view of the surrounding area.

In the distance lurked a dark, dark forest. A path led to the sparse eaves, about a three-minute walk from a wide river. A broken bridge sat in a permanent slump against the bank.

My villagers had driven their cart up from the south, which meant most of the southern section of the map was visible. The monsters came from the north, so my villagers tended to avoid that area as best they could.

"Wonder what kind of event this is..."

I'd run through countless scenarios in my head but gave up when I realized there was no use trying to solve a riddle without any clues. When I sent my prophecy detailing the event, I didn't bother to give my villagers an exact time. None of them had a watch. Unfortunately, this left my villagers restless the entire morning. I felt bad—I should have at least told them it would start a couple of hours before lunch.

"Everything's quiet right now, but I can't let my guard down."

My villagers gathered just inside the fence. Gams, the swordsman and the only one with any fighting ability, stood atop the watchtower, keeping a close eye on the surroundings. I zoomed out the mini-map as far as I could, but there wasn't any... Wait a second.

Was that movement in the north just now? I zoomed in to find a figure making its way towards the cave—a person. It was only when he stepped out of the forest and into the light that I recognized him—beautiful enough to be mistaken for a woman, with a bow on his back.

"Murus is back?"

Murus was the physician who left my village just before the Day of Corruption. I'd more or less seen it coming, but it still threw me when it happened. I *did* want him out of there though, so I hadn't been upset.

Gams was the first to spot Murus. He waved at him. "Murus!"

Murus waved back, but he didn't look particularly happy. My villagers, however, seemed relieved to hear the familiar name, and Carol even made her way up the ladder to stand next to Gams, waving her arms excitedly. Murus's face clouded for a split second, then cleared. He smiled back at her.

"So, what, is he like...a bonus character for the event or something? It'd be nice if he finally joined our village."

Judging from the look on Murus's face, that was wishful thinking. Also, gaining him back would be a pretty boring prize. I moved my cursor over Murus, but most of his bio was still hidden. The main event was clearly yet to come.

Gams slid down from the watchtower and raced up to the wooden fence. The slat at the end looked just like the rest at first glance, but it had a hidden door. Gams opened it to allow Murus in. The other villagers gathered around excitedly to greet him.

"Welcome back, Murus!" Carol clung to his waist, and he patted her head fondly.

"It's good to be back, and I'm happy to see you all looking so well. I'm sorry for arriving out of the blue like this after running away so selfishly." Murus bowed in apology, but no one looked displeased to see him.

"Nonsense. You helped us so much. We have a lot to be grateful for, don't we, dear?"

"That's right," Rodice said. "We're just glad you're here."

"Indeed," added Chem. "Your return must be a gift from the Lord Himself!"

This exchange was exactly why I loved my villagers so much, and one of the best things about this game. Every last one of my villagers was a kind, caring person. Though appearances were more subjective, I couldn't imagine anyone disliking their personalities.

"Thanks for your help on the Day of Corruption, too," Gams said. He must have been talking about the arrows that felled several of the monsters during the fight. If I noticed them, it wasn't a surprise that Gams did as well.

"Not at all. I apologize that I couldn't do more. I realize I am in no position to ask for help, but I require your assistance..." Abruptly, Murus sank to one knee and bowed his head.

Chem immediately darted forward to pull him back to his feet. That pose must have been the equivalent of getting on your hands and knees in the real world.

"Please raise your head, Murus. Not only did you save my brother, you helped us out in so many other ways. We shall assist you in any way we can. Isn't that right, Gams?"

"Yup. We owe you one, so just let us know what you need."

The other villagers nodded their agreement along with the siblings. Since I knew Murus's true identity, I was pretty conflicted—but he just needed a personal favor, I figured it should be fine. I wanted to believe that Murus himself was a good egg. And from a gaming perspective, this was an obvious chance to add him to my village once we cleared the special event.

"First," Murus began, "I want to clear the air. I am not simply a traveling physician who stumbled upon your village by chance. I belong to a group of settlers living in the Forbidden Forest."

Everyone besides Gams and Carol looked surprised. Gams had likely deduced there was more to Murus during the time the two spent together. Carol, meanwhile, probably had no idea what he was talking about.

"I see. Does that mean you already knew how much danger the Day of Corruption posed to those living here?"

Chem's question was unusually direct—no wonder, given the injuries her beloved brother sustained during the attack. She leaned forward with an accusatory glint in her eye, but Gams put a warning arm out in front of her. Pacified, she let out an awkward cough and took a step back.

"I'm sorry. I did know some of it. However, I did not foresee how dangerous it actually would be. The attacks came more regularly than usual, and the monsters' behavior was peculiar."

That made me curious. Since this was a video game, the regular waves of attacks made sense, but there might be something in the lore to explain it as well.

"I found it odd, too," Gams said. "Back in the village, we didn't get monsters attacking in mixed groups. I've never seen different species cooperate like that before."

Rodice added, "Hm, you're right. I used to venture out to sell my wares several times a year, and I've heard stories of monster attacks from all sorts of folks. But I'd never heard of hordes of monsters attacking an entire village before. When they worked together, it was never more than a handful at once."

I thought back to the game's opening cutscenes where those goblins rode up on boars. Apparently, that was unusual for this world. At the time, I'd just assumed that people rode boars here the same way they rode horses.

"Anyway, what did ya need help with?" Gams asked, bringing both me and the villagers back from our thoughts.

"My village was...destroyed on the Day of Corruption."

I heard a gasp, and I wasn't sure if it came from me or one of the villagers. Whatever I expected Murus to say, it wasn't that. Judging from Murus's words, his village seemed to have been around for a long time. Long enough to know how to deal with monster attacks, at least.

"Like I said before, this attack was different. Bigger than any we've ever faced, with different monster species working together. A survivor told me it was like they were being controlled by an outside force. The village chief sent me out into the forest to keep an eye on you, which was how I managed to escape the danger."

Murus averted his gaze. His shoulders shook, likely from the guilt of being unable to help his village.

"What about the survivors? Why not bring them here? We've got shelter, not to mention the God of Fate's protection."

Despite Murus admitting to spying, not one of my villagers reacted in anger. And not only that; they invited him to bring a bunch of strangers into their home. Perhaps they were being naive, but I liked that about my villagers. I would just have to be distrustful on their behalf.

I was all for the village gaining more people, too. Strength in numbers, etc. And Murus could keep them in check, right?

"I cannot thank you enough for your kind offer, Gams. But I am afraid they all lost their lives in the attack. When I got back, there was only one survivor...and he eventually succumbed to his injuries."

Wow, this was a grim scenario even for a game. If Murus's request was to join the village, I'd happily accept.

"The problem is...the number of bodies does not match the population. I am sure some might have been eaten, but still, there are dozens of children missing, and several adults. I am afraid the monsters might have dragged them off to their dens and nests." Murus mumbled all of this with his head down, making it impossible to read his expression.

I couldn't imagine being left behind as a sole survivor, forced to catalog all those dead bodies, every broken piece of the place I grew up. Murus's heart must be shattered. I was lucky to live in a country where that didn't happen.

"If there's even the tiniest chance that they're still alive, there's no time to waste. Let's go."

"I shall go and fetch some weapons," Chem said.

"We'll need food and water, too, lightweight and easy to carry. Lyra, please prepare us some flasks."

"Will do! Oh! Are you giving me a hand, Carol?"

"Uh huh! Everyone's helping out, right?"

The villagers wasted no time making preparations. They'd had their share of troubles and knew exactly what to do. Their indomitable spirits made even a deadbeat like me want to do everything in my power to protect them.

Murus stared, shocked that they'd agreed to his request so readily.

"After everything I kept from you...thank you. Thank you so much!" Falling to his knees again, Murus began to sob.

"That's just how wonderful my villagers are," I murmured aloud.

I really *was* proud of them. Hearing Murus speak so gratefully to them made me feel warm inside, as if he were thanking me, too. I decided to do whatever I could to help...as one of their own.

chapter 02 — The Rescue Plan and the Supportive God of Fate

THE VILLAGERS GOT TO WORK gathering everything they needed for the rescue. I considered my own options. I had the daily prophecy, but since I could only send one per day, I wanted to keep it for when I had something pressing to pass on. But I had plenty of Fate Points, so spending some on a miracle wouldn't be a problem.

I could summon a character, but there was no guarantee they would show up immediately. Plus, I had no idea what they would be like. I might just throw more trouble into the mix when everyone already had enough to deal with.

"I wish I could use the golem, but I'd probably run out of FP before we even got to where we're going."

I'd already used up all the FP I bought with my wages, and now all that was left were the points built up from my villagers' gratitude. I had enough to operate the golem but not for very long. Although, if my villagers could carry the statue part of the way... Nah, that was asking too much, even for someone as strong as Gams. I knew exactly how heavy wood could be from the logs they sent me as offerings.

"You guys don't mind leaving this trip to me and Murus, right?" Gams asked. "Just stay in the cave till we're back, okay?"

I agreed with Gams's judgment. He was the only capable fighter. Anyone else would just be a distraction.

"Please, let me join you. What if one of the children you rescue is injured?" Chem said.

"You make a good point, but I'd still rather you stay behind. It's too dangerous."

"I'm prepared for danger."

I wasn't sure how I felt about this myself. If this were any other game, sending a healer with the group was just common sense. Chem had training and could defend herself if need be, but I'd never actually seen her fight any monsters. She didn't have any weapons or armor, either.

"We have the God of Fate watching over us," she added, clutching her holy book to her chest.

If she was bringing that book with her, I'd be able to send a prophecy to them on their journey.

Wait, why I am worrying so much about this? The decision was Gams's to make in the end.

"I'm your brother, and I wanna keep you safe, but...I'm not gonna be able to stop you tagging along, am I?"

"Correct!" Chem giggled.

Gams let out a sigh, but his sister looked pleased as punch, like a child who'd pulled off a successful prank. I understood exactly where Gams was coming from. I felt protective of my sister, too. Still, if they found the surviving children, they'd have more non-combatants to worry about. Having someone else to take care of them when Gams and Murus were fighting would be a big help.

"If only I were stronger, I could come, too," Rodice lamented.

Don't look so down, Rodice. There's plenty for you to do in the village that doesn't involve fighting.

"Everyone has their job. We just have to do our best where we're most suited. Staying here and holding down the fort is just as important as going out and saving those children." Lyra gave her husband a powerful pat on the back.

He stumbled forward, only just managing to keep his footing.

"Gams, please take this! It's a special charm. You gotta protect it, just like you would protect me! Mommy said something this small won't get in your way!"

"Thanks. I'll take good care of it." Gams took the tiny wooden doll from Carol.

It was the same sort of carved doll that she sometimes sent me as an offering. Studying it closely, I could tell it was her best one yet. Though only thumb-sized, the face was carved with more detail than anything she'd sent me before.

"That's a super good one." I glanced over at my bookshelf, where I kept all the dolls she sent me. Those were hard to even recognize as people. Had her carving skills improved, or did she just expend more effort on Gams? Well, she did have a crush on him, so it was no wonder. I was on the verge of jealousy, but I guess true love isn't something you choose. Though Chem's hideously strained smile made me nearly reconsider my stance.

"Make sure you come home safe, Gams and Murus!" Carol called loudly, deliberately leaving Chem out.

I could practically see the veins bursting on Chem's forehead as her smile continued to widen. It was terrifying.

"I can't believe Carol's making enemies at her age! Though I guess she's just teasing Chem. She doesn't really know what she's doing, right?"

I couldn't be sure, though—I hadn't really spoken to a woman other than my mother or sister in years. Chem and Carol stared each other down, both somehow smiling and scowling at the same time. If this were a scene in a manga, the background would be full of writhing flames. I glanced away from the screen for a bit, leaning back in my chair to stretch. Once the group set off, I'd have to keep my focus on the game, so this was a good chance to get a quick drink and a bite to eat. I reached for the fruit on my plate—a new variety, as small as grapes but with a taste closer to apples. I felt around...but there was nothing there.

"Huh?"

I glanced under my desk, but it hadn't fallen on the floor.

Maybe I ate it on autopilot?

No, that was stupid. There were ten of them on my plate when I brought it up, and I couldn't eat *all* of them without noticing. I glanced around the room to see if they'd rolled off somewhere, which was when I saw it.

"Gaah! Wh-When did you get those?"

The newborn golden lizard had my fruit, its throat bulging as it swallowed one down. The lizard sat on the edge of my desk, its large eyes darting around the room as it stuffed its cheeks full. It was frustratingly cute. From my research, I'd already learned that some lizards liked fruit, and clearly this was one of them. I was relieved I wouldn't have to feed it any insects or mice. I hated the thought of handling anything like that.

"C'mon, you shouldn't be out of your tank. Oh, the glass on top shifted..."

I wanted to put the lizard back in the tank, but I wasn't sure if I should touch it. I didn't think it was gross or anything, but I was afraid of using too much force and crushing it—it looked so tiny and weak. I'd watched a ton of videos on keeping lizards, though, and quite a few of *those* people took them out of their tanks to pet them. And the scales on this one looked rough, so it might be me who ended up getting hurt if I handled it too much.

"All right, you can stay there as long as you behave yourself."

The lizard slowly nodded its head. Huh. Coincidence, or were reptiles smarter than I realized? Dogs could understand some words, so maybe some lizards or snakes could, too. I decided to ask Sayuki or Dad later; they were the real experts.

"Hey, I haven't given you a name yet. I'll give you one later. Just hold tight, okay?"

It appeared to nod again, but I decided not to dwell on that for now. I had the event to worry about. I turned back to the screen just in time to see my villagers stepping out through the log fence.

"We'll be going now. Please be careful while we're gone," said Chem.

"No need to worry about us. Once the cave door is closed, we won't take even a single step outside," Lyra said.

"Leave it to us," Rodice agreed, "and if things get too dangerous, please come back right away. Remember, there's a fine line between bravery and recklessness."

"We'll make you the yummiest meal ever for when you get back!" Carol promised.

Rodice's family saw the three off as they started on their way. According to the map, there was no immediate danger, but the northern section where they were headed was still completely hidden by the fog of war. Murus said he would tell them the details of what had happened on the way. I paid close attention.

"I am not sure how many monsters we will encounter. I found several monster corpses in the village, and some of them must have been driven away. I don't think there are many monsters left nearby."

"Hopefully any of those will be injured, too."

"I am familiar with many of the places monsters nest within the Forbidden Forest. Even my people don't know every nook and cranny of this place, but I do have detailed knowledge of the area immediately around the village. Three types of monsters live in the forest...and direwolves and boarnabies don't often carry their prey home alive. That leaves the green goblins."

I was impressed by Murus's knowledge. The goblins weren't much bigger than children themselves, and I couldn't imagine them carrying full-grown adults around. But little kids probably wouldn't give them much trouble. Still, the thought was gruesome.

"This isn't a Mature-rated game, is it? There was nothing about ratings in the manual, I don't think. This is making me nervous." I knew there were games out there with extremely graphic or cringey stuff like dead children or animals crossbreeding with each other. This game was hyper-realistic, so if something horrible happened, I doubted I'd be spared the gory details.

"Ugh, now the super-good graphics have me a little freaked out. I can't deal with anything too grotesque."

Saying this made me feel awful for Murus, considering what he had witnessed. I wondered what was going through his head right now. I knew this was all fictional, but I couldn't help imaging myself in his shoes. I wouldn't even have the courage to fetch help, let alone wander into enemy territory. Picturing my own villagers in the same situation, I wouldn't be able to dismiss it as just a video game. Even thinking about it made me feel sick and shaky.

At the moment, Murus was leading the group. I zoomed in on his face. He was staring straight ahead with a gleam of determination in eyes, chewing on his bottom lip. He didn't stop moving for an instant. I strengthened my resolve to focus and be ready for anything.

My first priority was making sure Gams, Chem, and Murus made it back safely. Next was finding the kidnapped children and rescuing them if possible. Finally, we would wipe out the monsters if we could. The moment my villagers tried anything too reckless, I would send a prophecy to stop them.

"So we're looking for green goblins?" Chem asked.

"Monsters do not cooperate with each other outside of the Day of Corruption," Murus replied. "When we went out scouting two months ago, we counted fifty-five goblins. I found around forty dead in the village. If some of the surviving monsters were seriously injured, those numbers might be off, but I believe we should expect around twenty goblins left at most."

I couldn't believe how precisely he answered her question. Not only did he count the bodies of his fellow villagers, he counted the monsters, too. Murus was a far stronger man than I.

"Twenty is a lot to take on alone. Good thing there are two of us," said Gams.

"Indeed. It's a great help to have somebody on the front lines," Murus replied, taking up his bow. I already knew how good an archer Murus was from his time spent with my villagers. I only saw him miss a shot once in the whole two weeks.

Suddenly, Murus held up a hand to stop the others. The three of them crouched.

"We still have a way to go before we hit their territory, but I already see two monsters. We should deal with them now," Murus whispered.

He muttered something, and the weeds in front of them grew tall and shielded them from view. I wasn't surprised that he could manipulate plant life with magic, but I was impressed by how deftly he did it. Without being touched, the weeds parted to allow my villagers to peer through. Murus quietly nocked two arrows on his bow, tilting it as he fired them simultaneously. The arrows embedded themselves in their victim's heads, and the goblins went down without a sound.

"Whoa!"

I, on the other hand, couldn't help but let out a gasp of admiration. I'd never seen such a perfect snipe. Gams approached the fallen goblins quietly and cut off the head of the one still breathing. I zoomed out while he did it, not wanting to see it in detail. Out of curiosity, I had once zoomed in to watch a monster being butchered, taking it all in. I couldn't stomach the meat we had for dinner that evening.

After hiding the bodies behind the same weeds they used for cover, the trio continued onward. They moved silently through the endless forest, but they didn't come across any more enemies.

"This is what we've been missing out on, huh?"

They'd been traveling through unexplored territory for a while now, and I still couldn't see what lay ahead on the map, only the path back from where they'd come. If Murus joined the village, the fog of war should clear and show me everywhere he'd seen around here, right? I kept checking and rechecking the map from overhead, even though I knew I couldn't see anything. Still, I watched. At the very least, if something tried to sneak up behind them, I could let them know.

They walked for another ten minutes before the area in front of them opened into a forest clearing. A large group of green goblins had made their camp here, their "buildings" nothing more than bundles of withered grass. The living conditions didn't look comfortable, but the goblins at least possessed the intelligence to build themselves somewhere to sleep.

No sign of any people at all, though. If they were here, they were likely being kept in those shabby shelters. My three villagers froze, tension running high between them. I felt it, too. I double-checked the miracles menu—open just in case—and held my breath as I waited for them to make a move.

chapter 03 — The God of Fate's Miracle and My Anxiety

I QUICKLY GAVE THE CAMP a once-over as I waited for my trio to ready themselves. Since my villagers were here, part of the clearing was visible on the map, as were eight or nine goblins. There were six structures labeled "huts" that were more like covered pits in the ground, probably large enough to fit around five goblins. Whether there were more enemies inside them lying in wait, or whether they held Murus's fellow villagers, remained to be seen. If we could confirm they only contained goblins, my group could set them alight with fire arrows. But there was no way to know.

"This is kinda frustrating..."

Our other option was to go in and pick the goblins off one by one, but since their camp was in a clearing, we'd probably be discovered immediately. If there'd been any grass or plants about, Murus could use his magic, but the space was just bare earth.

The lack of any defensive fences or walls made this place look deceptively easy to attack, but it also meant my group had nowhere to take cover. I racked my brain, thinking back over all the strategy games I'd played and books I'd read, but I didn't have a solution for this scenario. Waiting for nightfall would give them the cover of darkness, but there was no time to lose.

"Even havin' some cloud cover would be better than this," Gams grumbled up at the clear blue sky.

Right, if it were raining, visibility would be a little lower, but... Wait a second.

Why didn't I think of it sooner?

I saw it the first time I ever looked at the miracles menu: "Change the Weather." I'd figured it would come in handy if there was a drought, but it never occurred to me it'd be useful for something like this.

If it rained, my group would be more difficult to spot, their footsteps drowned out. The goblins might even retreat into their huts for shelter, making the whole attack easier.

No point in hesitating. I clicked the option to change the weather, opening up a second menu.

"*Blue skies, cloudy, light drizzle, rain, snow, torrential rain, heavy snow, blizzard, thunderstorm, typhoon.*"

"Damn, I'm spoiled for choice. Looks like some of these options are more expensive than others. The ones at the top are cheaper, and the ones at the bottom cost more."

The pricey options were *really* pricey, while the cheap ones were super reasonable. Blue skies, cloudy, and light drizzle were so cheap that I could use them frivolously. Rain was fine, too, but torrential rain was where the prices started to skyrocket.

I could afford everything except a typhoon.

"Maybe I should go for torrential rain? The goblins won't be able to hear a thing. I don't know if the regular rain will be enough for that."

If only I'd messed around with the weather before, I'd have a clearer idea of my options.

"Rain could also impact my group, though Gams did say he was hoping for some."

Every moment I wasted here was another moment the hostages could be killed, rendering this entire trip pointless. I had to make a decision. I took a deep breath and clicked on "torrential rain."

"Oh, looks like I have to pick how far I want my rain to reach. The bigger the area, the more it costs. The smallest I can pick is a circle with a diameter of five meters, and I can increase that a meter at a time... Okay."

The smallest size would just about cover the goblins' camp. I didn't want to make the supernatural nature too obvious, though, so I moved it up another meter. Right away, the sunlight faded, and the clearing fell into darkness. A few raindrops splattered the ground, and the next second, rain poured down from the sky. From above, I could make sense of the scene, but to anyone inside the storm, visibility would be nonexistent. As I expected, the goblins hurried inside their shabby little huts, anxious to get out of the rain. I checked around, but no enemies remained outside.

"To think the weather would change just as we were speaking of it," Murus muttered.

That's right, Murus! But this wasn't just a lucky coincidence.

"My book has been glowing slightly, Murus," Chem said. "I believe this is the work of the God of Fate. Seeing that we were in trouble, He came to our aid. Thank you, O Lord!"

Chem clung tightly to the book, protecting it from the rain with her clothes. I wasn't aware the book glowed when I was performing miracles, but at least it meant she knew this was my doing.

"I just hope it's enough..."

I knew that Gams and Murus were well trained, but I still couldn't help but be nervous.

"Could you take my stuff, Chem? I don't want it weighin' me down."

"Of course. Do be careful, won't you?"

Chem took the small bag and the other items Gams carried at his waist. Then, unburdened, he crept toward the closest hut. Putting his ear to the wall, he listened carefully. Murus readied his bow just in case, and Chem clasped her hands together in prayer. Gams peered inside a crack in the opening of the hut and, seeing it was empty, beckoned the others toward him. Their plan made sense—Gams would take the lead, and the other two would keep watch until he could confirm it was safe. If this were me and Sayuki, I'd probably come up with the exact same formation. If the worst had already happened, Gams going first meant he could spare Chem the sight of dead children.

"Though I sure hope the devs were nice enough not to put anything that horrible in here. You didn't, right, guys?"

Needless to say, there was no reply.

Leaving the vacant hut, Gams started moving toward the second. I'd seen two goblins go inside there when the rain started falling. I knew Gams saw them, too, because he was moving a lot more carefully than before. I stared at the screen, but no one emerged from the hut.

Once he was crouched beside it, Gams turned to the others and flashed a signal with one hand. They must have come up with the signals in advance, as only Murus moved forward when he saw it. Opening the entrance to the hut, the two crept inside. I listened as hard as I could, but everything was drowned out by the sound of the rain.

"Kinda weird how it won't let me see inside the huts," I grumbled to myself. Not that it changed anything. All I could do was sit back and wait impatiently.

Gams and Murus emerged again in less than a minute, covered in goblin blood that the rain swiftly started washing away. They were both shaking their heads—no children or villagers inside that hut either. Chem remained where she was as Gams and Murus attacked hut after hut, but they found no survivors. I saw one more dead goblin than the number outside before the rain started, meaning some of the huts had been occupied—just not by villagers.

"I guess we should be prepared not to find anyone," I said.

It was just a game, but I had come to treasure these people almost as much as my real family. I didn't want them to suffer tragedy or hardship. I longed only for their happiness, even if that made this the most boring game of all time.

Soon there was only one hut left, more than twice the size of the others. My group and I agreed this was probably the one we were looking for. Gams, Chem, and Murus made their way into the smaller hut beside it and peered out through a crack in the wall.

"Murus is so on edge, I hope he doesn't take any unnecessary risks. I don't know how long this rain is gonna last, either."

The miracles menu didn't say how long the weather would last, but hopefully it would be long enough for my group to achieve their objective. But I also didn't want them to rush. I could always just recast the rain miracle if I needed to. Even if it did use up more FP than I wanted, my villagers' gratitude would quickly earn it back.

For a while, the three of them were still. Then, they seemed to decide that they just had to go for it. Gams approached the larger hut first, leaving the door open behind him, where Murus waited with his bowstring drawn and ready to fire. Chem clung on to her book with everything she had.

Gams took one step, then another, the rain drowning out the noise. A few more steps, and he would be at the big hut's wall. But before he could make it, the door banged open.

Behind it stood not a green goblin but a creature at least a head taller than Gams. Its thick, ropey skin was bright red and looked like some form of natural armor.

"A *red* goblin?!"

The goblin held a club as long as a clothesline. It wasn't sharp, but it was so big that it could cause plenty of destruction, regardless. The goblin wore only a pelt around its waste, adding to its fearsome gravitas. But what stood out the most was its head. It had a single large eye, a mouth that spread impossibly wide across its cheeks, and no nose to speak of. This thing was so terrifying that *I* was trembling on the other side of the screen. Whatever it was, it was certainly a boss fight.

"I was wondering when something like this was gonna show up."

The creature glared down at Gams with its single eye.

"No way! A one-eyed red goblin!" Gams scowled, unsheathing his dual swords.

"What? A one-eyed red goblin mixing with green goblins?" Murus's eyes widened in surprise.

He quickly regained his senses and sent an arrow flying, hurtling straight toward the creature's huge eye. The goblin swatted it from the air like it was nothing. This wasn't going to be an easy fight. I clicked over.

"One-eyed red goblin: An incredibly savage and violent member of the goblin race. They hate green goblins and consider them enemies. Powerful beasts that the average hunter could never hope to defeat. They love the taste of human flesh."

Very informative, and very depressing.

If this thing liked to eat humans, our hostages might be long gone. But we couldn't focus on that right now. We had to take it down.

The goblin took a threatening stance and stared Gams down in the rain. The resentful air it gave off was almost suffocating. I was still trembling. If I were Gams, I wouldn't even be able to move.

The goblin swung its club down lazily, as if the human facing him was nothing more than an annoyance. Gams ducked, the strike missing so narrowly that his hair ruffled in its wake.

"One hit and he's dead."

Gams circled the giant goblin. He knew what I knew—if he stopped moving it would all be over. Murus continued to fire arrow after arrow at the creature, but it swatted them all out of the air like flies. I'd watched the two of them win battles together several times before, but my gut told me that this was an opponent they couldn't defeat.

Should I send them a prophecy and tell them to get out of there?

Gams was still circling and Murus still firing. They couldn't win under these conditions. As the God of Fate, I had to stop them.

Should I go for it or not?

I had to decide. Their lives depended on it.

chapter 04 — A Life-Threatening Battle and My Panicked Thoughts

THE RAIN CONTINUED to pour down. Gams darted at the goblin's side, striking out with his sword. The monster gave him a brief glance before slicing its club through the air, cutting the sheets of rain in half with a dull whoosh. Before I could register what had happened, Gams went hurtling backward, slipping across the soggy ground.

"Gams!"

I thought he was done for. But no, he'd blocked the attack with his sword, and now he was grimacing and sinking to his knees. He wasn't hurt, but the goblin saw that his balance was broken and advanced.

"Gams!"

This time, it was Chem who shouted for him. Beside her, Murus sprang into action. He fired more arrows, but the ones the goblin didn't swipe away simply bounced off its skin. Unbelievable—I'd seen those very same arrows slay monster after monster with a single strike.

"This thing's just too tough!"

The arrows were enough of a distraction to allow Gams to get back on his feet, but now I was even less hopeful than before. He only just managed to dodge the creature's last attack, and worse, it wasn't even trying. When it raised its club and swung down, allowing Gams only a split second to dodge, it smiled at every narrow escape. It carried on launching the exact same attack again and again, like a human trying to squash a mosquito. Gams tried desperately to close the gap and get a strike in, but the goblin's size and the length of the club made it impossible. Even if he did get close, the monster would just send him flying again.

"This one-eyed red goblin is not normal," Murus said. "It must be legend rank, or even higher. If normal arrows won't penetrate it, maybe poisoned ones will... Although, I'm not sure even *they* will work, especially with this rain."

I instantly knew what Murus was getting at. He was a physician, meaning he knew all about poisons, and poison arrows might give us a shot at victory. Except, chances were the rain would wash it away before it got into the goblin's bloodstream.

Maybe I should stop the rain...

Not just for the poison, either. The increasingly muddy ground was hindering Gams's movement. But on the other hand, the heavy rain battering the creature's eye lowered its visibility, which was good for us. Besides, it wasn't like stopping the rain meant the ground would dry up straight away. I felt like my best option was to send them a prophecy instructing them to run—but no, that might be even more dangerous than fighting at this point. The moment my group turned their back on the monster, they would be defenseless.

"What do I do?! I don't even have time to think! Ugh! What *can* I do?! What can I do right now?"

If only I had the golem nearby. Unlike on the Day of Corruption, I came here without any real backup plans. Maybe I really *should* have asked my villagers to carry the statue with them. But then, if that slowed them down and the hostages died, this whole plan would be for nothing.

I had two options—send a prophecy or perform a miracle. And the miracle might not even take effect immediately. The only one I *knew* would work straight away was weather manipulation. The group's sole assets were the poison arrows, Chem's book, and the small bag she took from Gams.

I racked every last corner of my brain for knowledge I knew I didn't have.

But there was a third option: I could tell Chem and Murus to run while Gams stayed behind. Gams was sharp—he would notice their flight immediately and probably stay behind to act as a decoy to let them get to safety.

Gams's life...didn't actually matter. This was just a game. They were just polygons. Nobody real was going to die.

But if I really believed that, then why was I so terrified?

"No. I'm getting everyone back alive. There's gotta be a way out of this! They wouldn't make a game that's impossible to win! There's got to be a way to turn things around!"

I knew full well that I'd squandered my potential, leaving myself with nothing to fall back on but random scraps of knowledge from anime, games, and manga. I had to know *something* that could help me now. *Some* detail I'd picked up in the last ten years!

What's the most effective way to deal with a situation like this?

I scrolled through my miracle options and ran through the available items, calculating our chances. Suddenly, a solution burst into my mind.

"Will it work?" I shook my head. "No. It *has* to work."

My fingers flew across the keyboard. I sent the prophecy as soon as it was ready.

"My book is glowing! I think the Lord is giving us some advice!" Chem pulled out the book and opened it straight away.

She read it quickly, then turned to Murus and gave him brief instructions. The two leapt into motion. I waited for Murus to ready his bow before opening the weather menu and decreasing the rain's area of effect, making it as small as possible. The downpour was localized around the goblin now, with Gams just out of reach. It was a startling sight, and Gams looked back at Chem—he must have realized this was a miracle. Chem signaled for him to back away from the goblin. He nodded and began to slowly retreat.

The goblin didn't appear to notice that it was now the only one being rained on. It continued to wave its club around, when suddenly its vision burst with light, followed by an echoing roar of thunder.

The goblin screamed.

The torrential rain was now a thunderstorm, and the club that it held so high became a lightning rod, bolts of electricity racing through it. The goblin stumbled drunkenly, smoke coming off its body.

"A lightning bolt didn't kill it?! This is insane!"

But it didn't matter. Murus had already fired his arrow. The goblin was bent backwards from the pain, its mouth open as it howled. Murus's arrow curved through the air and straight toward that open mouth, slathered with poison. As soon as it was down the goblin's throat, it would be game over.

But just as it looked like our victory was assured, the monster raised its giant hand and swatted the arrow away. It went from screwing its eye up in pain to reacting in a split-second. The corners of its large mouth curled into a mocking smile.

"Sorry, big guy."

Just before the creature's hand had stopped the arrow, an object detached from it—a small statue of the God of Fate, holding a tiny vial of poison. It flew over the monster's hand and fell, then ricocheted off the back of the goblin's hand and shot straight into its mouth. The goblin tried to slam its lips shut, but it was already too late. Controlling the little statue with the gamepad, I had it crush the tiny vial of poison in its tiny hand. The goblin swayed and fell to its knees, clutching at its throat. Then, it collapsed face first onto the ground.

Everyone held their breath as its body flailed in the mud, its movements steadily losing their force. In less than ten seconds, it went completely still.

"Yes! We did it!" I cheered, tossing my controller aside.

That plan could have gone so horribly wrong, but it worked! Considering it was something I came up with on the spot, I was pretty pleased. I'd be patting myself on the back for the whole rest of the day. My face burned with excitement, and I took a few deep breaths to calm myself down. I let my mind go back over my plan, grounding myself in the moment.

This was what I had written in that prophecy:

"I am going to create a thunderstorm focused on the one-eyed red goblin. As soon as lightning strikes it, fire an arrow into the monster's mouth. Before that, please give my tiny statue a vial of poison to hold and attach me to the arrow."

Not quite as divinely worded as usual, but I didn't have time to worry about that, and neither did Chem or Murus. As soon as I sent the prophecy, I used a miracle to activate the golem. Ever since seeing my statue come to life on the Day of Corruption, I'd been toying with an idea. If that statue counted as the "golem" simply because it was recognized as the God of Fate, did that mean I could control anything with my likeness? Then I remembered the tiny doll Carol gave Gams before they left.

Common knowledge held that lightning struck metal objects, but in truth, it just struck anything tall enough. When I forced the thunderstorm into such a small area, the tallest object around was that club, which I knew the goblin always lifted into the air before an attack. The monster was practically asking to be struck.

I'd been worried about hitting Gams, but fortunately he realized what I was doing and moved out of the way. Once the lightning struck the goblin, Murus took the opportunity to launch the arrow toward its mouth. The tiny statue clinging to it held a vial full of poison so powerful that a single drop could kill a boarnabie. I took control of the statue to ensure the vial landed in the goblin's mouth. I figured slathering poison on the arrowhead would be good enough, but it never hurt to be over-prepared, especially in rain like that. And it had all worked out in the end.

I would've loved to keep basking in our victory, but there were more important things to worry about. I checked the screen to find everyone gathered in one place. Chem's clothes were covered in mud; she must have raced up to her brother as soon as she could, uncaring of the puddles. She threw her arms around him and sobbed into his chest. Gams gently stroked her head.

The rain had stopped, and dazzling sunlight poured into the clearing. The gigantic monster lay dead in front of the three travelers. The tableau was heart-warming, almost dreamlike. I found myself staring at the screen for a while, forgetting everything around me. I wished I could celebrate along with them, but I'd already used up today's prophecy. I had to wait until tomorrow.

Besides, even if the battle was over, the mission wasn't. We still had to venture into that final hut.

chapter 05 — A Prayer of Peace and My Respectful Silence

AFTER THE ONE-EYED RED GOBLIN fell, no more enemies appeared. My group was safe. Still, I was careful not to let my guard down, checking around the clearing one more time.

"Looks like we're good."

Gams, Chem, and Murus stared silently at that one remaining hut. Their thoughts had to be all over the place. Murus was about to take a step forward, but Gams pushed to the front.

"I'll go look first. There might be more enemies wanderin' around."

"Very well. Thank you." Murus bowed his head quietly, his expression grim.

No doubt he burned with the desire to rush inside and see whether any of his fellow villagers were still alive. At the same time, terror at what he might find made him hesitate. *I* was so nervous that my chest felt tight, so I could only imagine how Murus must be feeling.

Gams picked his way carefully through the mud and approached the entrance to the hut. He listened carefully, and after a few seconds, deemed it safe, and snuck in. Frustratingly, I still couldn't see what was going on inside, but neither could Chem and Murus. All we could do was wait. I was still holding my breath when Gams reappeared. Seeing her brother was unharmed, Chem let out a sigh of relief and made to run towards him, but Gams held out a hand to stop her.

"You stay out here. I need Murus to see this."

His words and the anguished expression on his face left little doubt what was in there. Murus moved slowly towards him, his gaze glued to the ground.

"I'm a hunter, too, Gams," Chem said. "I'm ready for anything. Some of them might still be alive."

"I'm saying this as your brother. I don't want you seeing it."

That silenced Chem. She simply stood there, clutching her book to her chest.

After what could have been a few minutes, or perhaps only a few seconds, Gams and Murus emerged. Their expressions were dark. Chem didn't need to ask what happened.

"Thank you so much for accompanying me all this way," Murus said, bowing his head.

"I'm sorry we couldn't do anything."

"You don't need to thank us. Please, raise your head," Chem said kindly.

Murus couldn't even muster up a reply. He just stood there,

face down and shoulders trembling. Just watching him made my heart sting. I reached out for a tissue and wiped at my eyes and nose. I couldn't help but shed a few tears as I realized that could have been my village.

"Dammit!"

I remembered thinking as a kid that I would stop crying so much when I grew up, but now that I was in my thirties, it seemed to just be getting worse. Adults were brought to tears as often as kids were. They just had to grit their teeth and hold it in.

"Murus, would you mind if I prayed for your lost companions so that their souls might find peace?"

Murus looked up at Chem's gentle request, tears trailing down his face.

"Please...please do."

Gams cut a square out of the straw hut with his sword and went back inside. He was probably going to use it to cover the children's bodies, both out of consideration for the dead and so that Chem wouldn't have to see them. Murus and Chem followed him, and I watched them pray through the hole in the wall. I put my own hands together and wished that the children would find happiness in their next lives. I knew, logically, that it was just a game, but it was what my heart told me to do.

Next, the three of them dug some graves, and Gams and Murus took the disfigured bodies out for burial. Any other game would have cut this part out and restarted once the three made it back to the cave, but *The Village of Fate* was different. In this game, people lived, and people died.

None of them said a word as they trudged home, their footsteps heavy. The moment they were back inside the fence, Carol rushed up to them.

"Welcome back, Gams, Murus, and Chem!"

The cheerful smile on her face vanished instantly as she noticed their expressions. As much as they were trying to hide their distress, they clearly had no good news to share. Carol began to tremble. Lyra appeared to hug her from behind. Rodice put down his axe where he was chopping firewood and approached the three with a tender, sympathetic smile.

"Welcome back. You must be hungry after all that walking. I'll put something small together for you. Eat, and then get some rest."

He didn't ask them what happened. He simply did what he could to make sure they took care of themselves.

"Don't beat yourselves up, guys... You did really well..."

Watching Rodice handle the situation so compassionately made my eyes well up with tears again. What was Murus going to do now? I would love for him to join us, but that was a decision he would have to make for himself. If he wanted to go off and live on his own for now, I wouldn't have the right to stop him. I decided to keep an eye on him for now. Currently, he was sitting in one of the small rooms staring blankly at the ceiling. I didn't want to leave him alone.

"Yoshio! Dinner's ready!" Mom called from downstairs.

I looked away from the screen. "I didn't realize how late it was."

I quickly glanced back to see what my villagers were up to. Murus was sitting against the wall with his eyes closed. He must be exhausted, both physically and mentally.

"I guess I can let him sleep for a little while."

I came downstairs to find my whole family at the dinner table.

"Hey, I replied to your text. Didn't you see it?" Sayuki asked before I even sat down.

My sister was still in her work clothes, minus her jacket. She seemed to be in a bad mood; she was talking to me like she used to before we started repairing our relationship.

"I was kinda busy today. I haven't looked yet."

"Seriously? After you sent me a photo of your cute little lizard and everything?"

"Oh."

Come to think of it, I *had* sent both Sayuki and Dad a photo of the newborn lizard to see if they could identify it. Sayuki must be crabby because I never acknowledged her reply. I didn't even check to see if Dad replied to me or not. I glanced at him. His expression was sterner than usual, and he was staring at me.

Looks like both of them are mad...

The event had completely obliterated any thought of the lizard from my mind, and I only remembered it now because my sister reminded me. Sayuki didn't need to be *this* mad, though. She was pouting and glaring at me. And hang on, did she just call the lizard "cute"? No, that wasn't like her. I probably misheard.

Oh, wait. I never put the lizard back in its tank.

"Yoshio? Where are you going?"

"Oh, um, I left my phone on my desk. I wanted to go get it in case work calls me..." Garbling my excuse, I turned around to go back to my room, only to find the lizard sitting at the bottom of the staircase.

"Hey!"

What was it doing there? And...was it just me, or did it seem much bigger? It looked twice the size it did when it came out of its egg. I didn't know reptiles could grow so quickly.

"Ah! Is this the little cutie?"

I'd never heard Sayuki use such an adoring tone before. She rushed up to the lizard. A low scrape came from the dining table, and I glanced over to see my dad half out of his chair before sitting back down again.

"Oh, wow! It really is gold! I thought it was just the lighting in the photo. You know, you get Japanese skinks and grass lizards that are a kinda golden color, but not as golden as this! What do you think, Dad?"

"Hmm. Let me take a look."

Sayuki immediately scooped up the creature into her arms and brought it to Dad, absolutely beaming. I was kind of scared, to be honest; I'd never seen her this excited about anything before.

"With the size and the sharp scales, I'd say it looks like an armadillo lizard if it weren't for the color. Maybe it's a new mutation? The back legs are abnormally thick, too."

Even with their love of reptiles, they weren't sure exactly what it was. They continued their eager discussion, curiosity bright in their eyes.

"You can talk about the lizard all you want after dinner. Let's just eat for now," said Mom. "Oh, but Yoshio, did you name it?"

"Not yet."

"Well, come up with something soon. We can't welcome it into the family until it has a proper name!"

Mom seemed to have taken a liking to it, too. I'd have to be sure not to make the name too cringey.

"By the way, Oniichan," Sayuki said, "do you know what it eats yet?"

"I didn't get any instructions, but it was eating some of that fruit from the village earlier."

"Huh, that's odd. Lizards usually eat bugs or meat."

Sayuki could probably go on for hours, but Mom was getting more and more impatient with us now.

"I'll just put it back in my room."

I took the lizard from Dad and Sayuki, who both looked sad to see it go. I rushed to put it back in the tank in my room.

"Sorry, but you'll have to stay here for a bit."

The lizard stared at me with its big eyes. This time, though, it didn't nod.

"Please? I'll bring you some extra fruit later if you behave."

Now it nodded vigorously.

It couldn't understand me...right? Maybe reptiles just had a habit of moving their heads up and down. In fact, I was pretty sure I saw them doing that on TV.

"I'll be back after dinner, so stay in your tank," I repeated before going back downstairs.

No one had started eating yet; they must have been waiting for me. I sat down hurriedly.

"Let's get started," Mom said.

After what happened with *The Village of Fate*, I'd completely lost my appetite, but talking about the lizard with everyone brought it back again. I cleared my plate. I was headed back to check in on Murus and everyone, when I realized I was being followed.

"Can I see it again?"

"You'll need our advice, won't you?"

Those were questions, but they weren't asking.

"Okay..."

I guess it's fine to leave this to the experts.

I quickly checked on the village before letting them in, but nothing had changed over dinner. I minimized the application before opening the door for my father and sister. As soon as I put the fruit into the tank, the lizard bit it hungrily.

"Awww! Look at it eat! It's so cute!"

"Yes, it's lovely."

Dad and Sayuki practically had their noses pressed up against the glass. Mom said they liked reptiles, but I wasn't expecting them to like them *this* much. I doubted I'd get to hear the "advice" Dad offered any time soon. While I didn't love that I was now being ignored, I didn't feel as down as I did before, and it was all thanks to my family and a lizard.

Thanks, guys...

chapter 06 The Calm in the Village and the Storm in my Mind

SAYUKI AND DAD were still in my room, fawning over the lizard.

"Maybe you should turn up the temperature and humidity in there a bit."

"Ah, armadillo lizards like to sunbathe on rocks. You should change the layout of the tank a little and add a shelter."

"Right, but what about the flooring? And the light in there is one of those new ones..."

I only understood around ten percent of what they were saying. Well, as long as they were having fun.

"Did no one tell you what kind of lizard it is, Yoshio? I'm *pretty* sure it's an armadillo lizard, but I'd like to be certain."

I jumped, not expecting either of them to talk to me. Luckily, I had a story prepared for this very question.

"Right, well, remember that I was helping out this village with its development projects? You know, the village up in Hokkaido?"

"Yes."

"Yeah."

They both answered at the same time, their eyes still firmly fixed on the lizard. A memory of Dad telling me off for talking to someone without looking them in the eye suddenly surfaced.

"Anyway, as part of that project, they've been doing some selective breeding to create new species to become the symbols of their village. That's how this lizard was born, and it's the same deal with those fruits."

It was only partly a lie—hopefully that would give it more credence.

"Please try to keep this little guy a secret. Same with the fruit. Don't go spreading those photos around."

I'd seen them taking photos this whole time, but now they attempted to hide their phones behind their backs. They were totally planning to show their photos to everyone.

"The village wants me to find out what it eats apart from fruit and whether it can be kept in a regular household like this."

"If it's a new species, it needs to be registered, and you probably need permission to keep it," Dad mused. "I suppose the village has sorted all of that out for you. I don't know too much about that area of things, to be honest."

I nodded, knowing full well that the village had probably done no such thing. I was starting to get angsty about the state of said village, so I ushered my visitors out of the room. They stared at the lizard longingly as they went, and I locked the door after them. No one ever came into my room if the door was closed, but I didn't trust that now that I had a lizard they were so in love with. I made a mental note to switch off my monitor when I went for a bath.

Alone at last, I sat down at my desk. With so much happening in the real world, I nearly forgot about the tragedy in-game, but my villagers sure hadn't. They were passing the time quietly in their rooms. Carol was asleep, her parents seated beside her, gently stroking her hair.

"I feel awful for Murus. We were driven from our village, too, but we still have our family."

"I know. They say that time heals all wounds, but that doesn't make it easy. I just hope Murus can recover eventually."

These villagers knew the pain of losing their home and the people around them, just like Murus had. I checked on Chem and Gams. Gams was out like a light after the exhausting day, and Chem was trying to pray, but she kept dozing off halfway through. Even if she hadn't fought like her brother, she walked all that way and helped dig the graves. That was tiring enough in itself.

"Don't worry about praying to me, Chem. Just get some rest."

Murus had moved from the floor to his bed, but his eyes were wide open as he continued to stare at the ceiling.

"I wonder what he's thinking right now... I just hope he doesn't do anything drastic."

He'd lost the will to live, but I needed him to fight through it as best he could. I wondered who he might have lost. Maybe his family or his lover. He looked young but still old enough that he might've had a wife and children. Being single myself and, until recently, entirely mooching off my family, it felt presumptuous to say I knew how he felt. I *was* extremely worried for him, though. He kept getting up from his bed and picking up the dagger he'd left on the floor. Anxiety bubbled up in the pit of my stomach every time he touched it, but without any way to stop him, I could only watch.

On second thought, I *could* activate the golem and intervene. Part of me wanted to respect his choice, but the part that wanted to keep him alive was stronger.

Another hour passed. Murus took a book out of his physician's bag of herbs and medicine. He scanned the green cover and let out a sigh.

"Why didn't you save us? The God of Fate managed when we needed *Him*." He scowled, but there was more anguish in his expression than anger.

I guessed that book was much like the one Chem carried but for the God of Murus's people instead. Unlike our book, which I could send messages to, theirs was probably inert. My villagers were always so moved and surprised by my prophecies that it made me think the communication I had with them was unique.

To be blessed by a god in the game world seemed to be a miracle in and of itself. Murus watched the God of Fate perform miracles right in front of him—no wonder he was feeling resentful towards his own God.

"Hey. Wait a sec."

Suddenly, horror filled me as I realized there was nothing stopping *me* from abandoning my village. If they were attacked while I was at work, I wouldn't be able to do a thing. The entire village could be destroyed without them seeing a single miracle. Exactly what happened to Murus's people.

"Now that I'm working three or four times a week, it's a definite possibility."

So, what? Should I just quit my job and go back to being a NEET?

I can't do that.

I couldn't throw it all away—it took me so much effort to get here. If only there was some way to keep an eye on my villagers even when I was at work. I scrolled through the options screen without much hope, but a button piqued my interest.

"Download the app for access to *The Village of Fate* wherever and whenever you want!"

There was an app?! This wasn't my first time looking through the game options, but I must've missed it before. Since Mom gave me her old smartphone, I could actually use apps now. I downloaded it straight away, and soon the familiar *The Village of Fate* logo appeared on the screen.

"Looks like I can perform miracles and write prophecies from my phone, too."

Perfect. I wasn't going to start checking my phone while I was supposed to be working, but now at least I could keep track of things on my breaks or in the car on the way home. It was a real load off my mind.

I checked my FP. It had gone up after our fight with the goblin, my trick with the doll, and our victory ensuring my villagers' gratitude. Of course, I didn't get back all the points I used, only about a third. Enough for a few miracles.

I wasn't sure what Murus planned to do, but I would offer him a miracle anyway.

The sun woke me up. As soon as my eyes were open, I sat down at my PC to check on Murus. He wasn't in his room. I moved to the wobbly homemade table to find all my villagers sitting there… along with Murus. Breakfast was being served.

"Thank God." I breathed a sigh of relief.

He wasn't smiling, but I was glad just to see him alive. Gloom hung heavily as everyone ate. Even Carol was quiet. She didn't understand what was going on, but she was smart enough to read the room.

"Sorry to make you go through all this trouble," Murus said, putting his cutlery down beside his barely touched plate of food.

"There's no need to apologize."

"I gave this a lot of thought last night, and I won't force the issue if you aren't comfortable with it," Murus began. "But I wonder if I could stay here with all of you. I considered leaving this place for good, but there might still be some survivors out there. Besides, I know absolutely nothing about the world outside the forest. This is the only home I know."

I found myself grinning slightly. This was just what I'd hoped for, but more than that, Murus's request showed he'd decided to keep living. The other villagers exchanged only a quick glance amongst themselves before breaking into smiles.

"Of course you can stay. Why would we refuse?"

"I agree with my brother. We'll be glad to have you."

Murus took Gams's and Chem's extended hands.

"You're gonna live here?! Yay!" Carol cheered, leaping up and down.

"It's so lovely to see our numbers growing, don't you think, dear?"

"Yes," Rodice agreed, "and we're happy to have you, Murus."

"I knew you guys wouldn't let me down." I smiled at my villagers' welcoming attitude.

"Murus has joined The Village of Fate!"

The message flashed up on the screen, officially marking Murus as one of my villagers. I clicked on him, finally able to read his bio.

"Murus, 151. Female. An elf who lives in the Forbidden Forest. A proficient archer and physician. Used to believe in the God of Medicine, a minor god under the God of Plants, but lost her faith when her village was destroyed."

"Huh..."

This was all unexpected, to say the least, but the parts that most caught my attention were her age and her race. Was she really 151?! By human standards, she looked in her twenties at most. Elves were generally known for their long lives and youthful looks, though, so it tracked. Her ears were hidden beneath her hair, and I couldn't tell if they were long and pointy. Thinking back, I *did* remember her saying something nasty about dwarves.

Plus, she was an archer who lived in a Forbidden Forest. It didn't get more elfish than that.

I should have noticed from the start. But this was a time for celebration, not frustration at my own ineptitude.

Oh, right—and apparently Murus was a girl? She was definitely pretty for a boy, but from her behavior and speech, I always assumed she was male, even if she never confirmed it.

"I guess Chem and Carol didn't notice either, though."

If they had, surely Murus would face far more resistance when attempting to hunt alone with Gams. If the doting sister and the young admirer ever teamed up, I couldn't even imagine how much damage they would do.

Anyway, Murus was one of us now. A single addition to our little family, but an important one. She knew how to fight, and she knew the forest and how to survive it. Not only that, but my villagers were already comfortable around her. I couldn't have asked for a better recruit.

"Welcome to the village, Murus."

In the light of everyone's smiles, a hint of color returned to her face. I only wished I could be there with them.

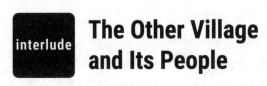

The Other Village and Its People

interlude

ONE MORNING, I received an important task from the village chief himself.

"A few days ago, some humans arrived in the Forbidden Forest. I want you to keep an eye on them to discern whether they pose a threat."

I set to work preparing for my task.

"It has been a long time since humans last came here," I murmured to myself.

Years...no, decades, by my count. We elves had lived here for thousands of years. Many violent monsters called this forest their home, and that tended to keep humans away. It was just us, the monsters, and a third group I didn't like to talk about. Once, dwarves and humans banded together to mine in the mountains, but the threat of the monsters soon drove them away. We'd lived in relative peace ever since, but now the humans were back.

No way to tell what they were like yet, but humans were often bad news. My first task would be to slip in among them and discover what they wanted here.

I hid my long ears under my hair and dressed in slightly shabby clothes. I heard that humans were often unsophisticated, particularly the men. I made sure every part of my skin was covered, ensuring they wouldn't be able to tell I was female.

There, that should make me look human enough. Doing this was humiliating, but this job was more important than my dignity.

My preparations complete, I left my village behind. My parents and the other villagers were worried about my youth—I was barely over a hundred—but they didn't need to be. I had confidence in my archery skills and medicinal knowledge. I was advanced for my age. The village chief must have thought so, too, or he wouldn't have chosen me.

Okay, truth be told, I was a *little* scared of the humans, but I was an elf! We lived in the Forbidden Forest long before they ever came along. *This should be no more difficult than frying an egg.*

I messed up.

While on my way, I saw a sudden pillar of light and followed it straight to the humans. Thinking on my feet, I told them I was a traveling physician. They bought it, but somehow I ended up playing along all the way to showing them a safer place to live.

I might have made a mistake, but my job was just to gather information, right? At least now I knew where they were.

Right! I did a *good* job!

This was all to gain their trust and extract more valuable information. Patience was key in matters of subterfuge, after all, and we elves were the most patient creature you'd find for miles.

Besides, even if they were human, I couldn't just up and leave when one of them was injured; I was a physician. If they showed any hostility, I would escape immediately, but they honestly didn't seem like bad people. I wasn't about to let my guard down, but...I wouldn't have known how sweet and innocent humans could be if I never met Carol. Don't get me wrong, though! All animals are cute when they're babies, and maybe humans were the same. I wasn't about to *ally* myself with these people.

I spoke with them often but found no evidence of ill intentions. The village elders always talked about how evil mankind was, but I was beginning to have doubts. They all saw that one traveling merchant as the single exception to the rule, but these humans seemed friendly, too. And as I watched them struggle to survive, I began to find it difficult to regard them as enemies.

Despite this, I continued to give my village regular reports on their movements. When I mentioned I thought these humans were good people, I was scolded and told that humans were masters of trickery and wordplay. I understood then that these humans must have simply ensnared me in their spell.

The elders told me that when they were young, they themselves were tricked by humans, and the outcome brought unspeakable misery. I had to remember not to let my guard down from now on. At the same time, I had to ensure they wouldn't suspect me, and therefore continued to treat them kindly and behave dependably. In their eyes, I was a skilled physician. As long as I kept up that persona, I could hold on to their trust and learn more.

I can do this!

Even among these uncouth creatures, I wouldn't forget that I was an elf. No matter how cute their young might be. If they posed a danger to us, it was quite possible I would be ordered to kill them. But that wasn't going to happen...right?

On the third day, the poisoned human recovered. Even an elf would struggle against the powerful venom of a direwolf's fang. He had to be strong, both in mind and spirit.

I often went out hunting with him. Unlike elves, who favored long-distance combat with a bow, he excelled at melee combat. His way of fighting complemented mine, and our hunts were far more successful than I would have expected. He wasn't talkative, so extracting information was difficult, but spending time with him wasn't a hardship.

He had a serious glint in his eye that could be off-putting, but he also possessed qualities that set him apart from the elf men I knew. Elves were beautiful and graceful. He was not, but perhaps wild men like him were not so bad after all.

That said...I often felt closely watched when I was with him, only to turn around and find that young religious woman smiling at me sweetly. Soon after, I spotted the icy glare in her eyes.

I was worried. Had she realized who I was? So far, no one behaved as if they suspected me, but maybe this human was particularly adept at hiding her suspicions. Like the elders said, I had to keep my guard up.

Humans were tricksters, I tried to tell myself, although I couldn't bring myself to extend the same label to little Carol. If the worst happened, perhaps I could bring her back to my village and care for her there.

Before long, the Day of Corruption arrived, the day that marked when the Corrupted Gods dared to rise up against our Major Gods. The threat was never severe, but lately the forest monsters had been acting strangely. They'd even started to band together to attack our village. They'd become so violent, and I longed for the days when our village walls could keep us safe.

It wasn't just the monsters' increasing ferocity that worried me, either. If they were forming groups, someone must be organizing them. Some intelligence was ordering them to attack all at once. We hadn't ever dealt with that before.

The mastermind could be a heretic or just a monster with unusually high intelligence. But every month the injuries and deaths in my village increased. I prayed to the God of Medicine as hard as I could that the village would pull through again this month.

The humans were aware of the approaching Day of Corruption, and I could sense their unease as their restlessness increased.

The cave they lived in was uncomfortable, but it at least offered some shelter, protected by thick planks of wood, surrounded by a fence made of logs. That was fine for everyday defense, but I feared it wouldn't hold up against the most dangerous day of the month. The humans felt the same way—they weren't fools, after all, and only one of them could hold his own in a fight. I imagined they were hoping I'd aid in the defense, though so far no one has asked me to.

I was just here to observe them. I had no obligation to help. On the contrary, things would be easier for me if they died. I could go home and tell my fellow elves we no longer had anything to worry about. It was the ideal outcome—but it didn't *feel* that way. Spending so long with them had clouded my judgment.

The village chief wanted me to come home, concerned over my wavering loyalties. The longer I spent here, the more I wanted to stay. Maybe their deceptive tactics really were working on me. I was confused. Lost. I didn't know what to do.

Please, Lord. Show me which path I should take.

They never encouraged me to leave, but when I said I was going, they didn't try to stop me. Only thanked me and kindly saw me off.

I wasn't abandoning them, just following my village chief's orders. The Day of Corruption was nearly here, and he needed me back as soon as possible.

I told him I would return once I knew if the humans made it through the Day of Corruption. He was reluctant but agreed. Many of the villagers were better archers than I; my people had many gallant fighters. They wouldn't miss me for just this month.

I wasn't staying back to observe the humans out of concern or pity. As an elf of the Forbidden Forest, it was my duty to watch them meet their demise. That was the lie I told myself.

But I had to accept it... I was *happy* with the humans. I enjoyed every day I spent with them and felt at home. So much so, that I found myself wishing I could stay there forever. But I couldn't turn my back on my village. I resolved that until the day came when humans and elves could finally understand each other, I would be the bridge that connected the two races.

That could wait until the Day of Corruption was over. I couldn't just go back and say I changed my mind, so instead I would focus on sniping monsters with my bow to thin out the numbers a bit. Should the humans survive, I would go and apologize for everything.

May we get through this, my friends.

To say I was surprised was an understatement. I couldn't believe my eyes when the God of Fate possessed that wooden statue. It struck down monster after monster, its movements as graceful as a dancer's. I couldn't look away. Was that *really* the God of Fate? Thanks to his miracle, the humans were able to overcome the Day of Corruption. I was jealous. The God of Medicine used to look over our village, too, and we received many prophecies, though not as often as these humans did. Still, I witnessed first-hand the kind of miracles our God was capable of.

But the last prophecy was months ago. Since then, we hadn't received any communications or seen any miracles. Nobody said it out loud, but we were all thinking the same thing: Our God had abandoned us.

I took my holy book from my bag. As usual, the page I opened was blank. He had sent no messages. What was the difference between us and the humans? Did we do something to upset our God?

Please, God, if you are still watching over us, give me a sign...

I prayed but received no response. I put the book away and headed back toward the village. I had to tell them that these humans were people we could trust.

"Wh-why?"

I returned to find my village destroyed.

I fell to my knees, the smoke stinging my nostrils. The sturdy fence that had protected the village for hundreds of years was utterly demolished, leaving the village defenseless. The plaza, once famed for the beauty of its multicolored flowers, was trampled and stained red with blood. No building was left untouched; most of them didn't even have roofs anymore. Elf and monster bodies lay scattered across the ground, disfigured and half-eaten, the awful creatures feasting in their victory.

"Is...Is anyone still alive?! It's me, Murus! Please! Someone say something!"

This has to be a nightmare!

I balled my hands into fists and struck them against my folded legs. Somehow, I managed to stand. I rushed through the village, calling out the names of its inhabitants. I searched for my noisy childhood friend who lived next door, the young thirty-year-old child from the same neighborhood, the village elders...but there was nobody left.

"Somebody say something, please! Please! Anyone!"

I called name after name until my throat was raw, but no one called back to me. I didn't give up, pushing my way through the rubble and checking every last building. My fingers were wet with blood, my skin slippery with sweat, and my body trembled with exhaustion, but I still continued to search for survivors.

"M-Murus? Is that you?"

A weak voice called out to me.

Was that the village chief?!

I raced toward the voice, pushing through the collapsed roof separating us. Underneath lay the village chief, spattered with blood.

"Chief..." I started, but my throat was so dry I couldn't continue.

"You do not need to speak. I will not survive this. Please do not exhaust yourself further on my account." The chief laid his hand over mine and shook his head as I tried to move the beam that crushed him. "Listen to me, Murus. The village is gone. However..."

I buried the villagers silently, one by one. I was afraid I would collapse before I could dig all the graves, but as a race with such a long life span, it was customary for elves to prepare their own resting places while they were still alive. In the end, I only had to dig graves for the children and adolescent elves. Carrying the bodies was also easier than I expected. Often I was only dragging pieces of my fellow villagers, large parts of their bodies torn away and devoured by the monsters.

Finally, I put the village chief to rest and let out a deep sigh. I put my hands together to pray for their peaceful rest. I wanted to hold a proper funeral, but there was something I needed to do first. I thought of it as I carried everyone to their graves. Clearly, some of the bodies were missing, even when accounting for a miscalculation due to the state of the corpses. The children especially appeared to be absent. The village chief told me with his last breath that some of them had been taken by the monsters.

I could grieve and cry later. Right now, I needed to take up my weapons and go. As a survivor of my village, I had a new task, one more important than shame or honor. So long as the possibility of survivors existed, I had to try.

part 5

MOVING FROM THE PAST

INTO THE FUTURE ↵

THE NPCs IN THIS VILLAGE SIM GAME MUST BE REAL! ↵

chapter 01 — My Childhood Friend and My Regrets

JUST AS I was about to let out a sigh of relief at Murus joining my village, I remembered something super important.

"Shit! I've got work at noon!"

I pulled on my coveralls as quickly as I could and rushed downstairs. Not only did I get up later than usual, I spent the whole morning on the computer! The carpool wasn't due to get me yet, but I hadn't had breakfast, let alone lunch. I had to eat something now or I wouldn't have another chance before dinner. Mom was nowhere to be seen, so I decided to fry up some of that boar-like meat from the village, which we had plenty of.

"It sure was nice of them to share their meat with us, but I never expected them to send a whole freakin' pig!"

My village killed more than ten of the monsters on the Day of Corruption, the majority of which they smoked to keep for later. With all that meat, they were set for most of the winter. They were clearly certain of that, because they proceeded to offer an entire boarnabie at the altar, which showed up in pieces at my house the same day. The poor delivery guy carrying that box was dripping with sweat.

I thought back to the moment I opened it to find it packed to the brim with meat.

Mom clapped her hands together in joy. "Oh, we won't have to buy any more meat for a month!"

Guess I can't complain, then.

I finished up the meat and added a little sauce. A simple meal but, as expected, delicious. Boarnabie was chewier than pork but surprisingly tender when cooked. Although the taste and texture were great, the delicious fat was what truly set it apart. It had a subtle sweetness and was less greasy than you'd expect. My internal food critic satisfied, I quickly demolished the meat on my plate.

"Seems like they can send whatever they want as an offering but only one type of gift at a time."

I thought back to when my villagers tried to send me a whole bunch of different fruit. Only the most plentiful variety disappeared and showed up at my house, the rest remaining behind on the altar. Additionally, they couldn't send me an endless supply of anything. They once tried three whole logs at a time but only managed to get one to me. I figured there was a weight limit, though I still had no clue how the offering system worked. I was tempted to experiment, but I couldn't just ask my villagers to send me a bunch of stuff out of idle curiosity.

"Delicious as always. Wonder if the car's here yet..."

The doorbell rang just as I said that. I put my dirty dishes away in the sink and headed out the door. I was super grateful I got to carpool to work. I knew most people hated commuting, and I was glad I didn't have to do it.

"Sorry I wasn't out right away."

"It's no problem at all! Right, Yama?"

My senior coworker sat in the back of the minivan. His name was Yamamoto-san, and as usual, he was playing a game on his phone.

"Hello," I said.

"'Sup."

He was usually smiling, but today he seemed a little down. Well, not so much *down* as grumpy, I guess.

I let him be, turning my attention to the view outside the window, only to catch him staring at me in the reflection. Did he want me to ask?

"Uh, is something wrong?" I tried.

"Mind if I vent?"

"N-not at all."

I was taken aback by his bluntness. I only asked out of politeness, really. I wasn't expecting him to want to just unload like that.

I guess even people like Yamamoto-san can't be happy all the time.

"Remember when I was tellin' you a while back about that game I was hooked on?"

"I do, yes. You said it was pretty unique, right?"

"Yeah, that one. The game where you're s'posed to invade and take over the enemy's territory. Well, I mean it's more complex than that really, but... Anyway, there was an event a bit ago that I spent my whole day off on, and I managed to capture this huge chunk of territory. But then yesterday, I lost a bunch just out of nowhere."

Oh, it was a *game* that had him so upset. Thank God. I'd been worried I wouldn't be able to relate to his woes, but gamer pain I absolutely understood. Even if I couldn't offer any advice, he had my full sympathy.

"I spent loads of money upgrading my monsters, but it didn't even matter. I guess I should just be glad I've got some land left, but I used up half of last month's paycheck on this stupid game."

Okay, now I knew *exactly* how he felt. Most of my paycheck went to microtransactions, too. Sounded like he was playing an online conquest game or something. I played similar things back when I was a NEET but gave up quickly when I realized most of them were pay-to-win. I'd spend a week building up my territory, only to be overtaken by some guy who made the same progress in one day just because he spent a crap ton of money. It was less fun for us free-to-play peasants.

"I...actually know exactly how you feel. I'm playing a game with microtransactions right now, too, and I lost tens of thousands of yen in an event the other day." I kept my voice down as I told him. I didn't want our boss to know this was where my paycheck was going.

"You did?! Man, I'm glad I told you! Let's not give up, but... let's try to keep from sinking in *too* much money."

"Right!" I shook his outstretched hand firmly.

A friendship built on the shared suffering at the hand of microtransactions. Maybe not a *healthy* foundation, but it was nice having someone to relate to. I wanted to know more about the game he was playing, but I didn't push. I didn't want to risk getting into something else and being tempted to abandon my villagers. Right now, all I wanted to focus on was *The Village of Fate*.

I was on vacuum duty again today. I was getting more and more used to the work, but my pride still got in my way. I had trouble gathering the courage to ask my coworkers or boss when I needed help. I'd read tons of posts online complaining about bosses snapping at employees to "use their brains" whenever they dared ask a question. My workplace wasn't like that, though. My coworkers were always willing to drop what they were doing to help me out.

"I'm glad Yamamoto-san cheered up."

I was worried when I first got in the minivan, but he seemed back to normal now. He was as hardworking as usual, his gloom dispersed. His personality was lackadaisical, but his work was perfect. Even the few times he got in trouble didn't affect the boss's confidence in him.

Work went smoothly, and our boss dropped me off outside the convenience store. It was late but not nearly as late as it would be if I'd worked night shift. A couple more buses would come through before the last one. I hurried into the store to escape the winter cold.

"Nothing like a meat bun when it's dark and chilly out..."

As I went through the store, I spotted some things I fancied buying, but Mom would have dinner ready for me at home, so I just picked up some dessert. I grabbed four puddings—my family all loved those.

Idly, I recalled meeting Sayuki here when that weirdo was hanging around the bus stop. I was still frustrated that she stopped me and let him get away. Since then, if my sister was coming home late, I came to meet her. She still felt like someone was watching her, some days. If the culprit wasn't caught, who knew when she would feel safe again? Puddings in hand, I stared out the glass front of the store, but there was no one out there.

I paid and pulled out my phone before leaving the store. I barely knew how to use the thing, and I always forgot to check it. Recently, I'd made a conscious effort to get into the habit. I checked the *Village of Fate* app more often than my messages, though.

"All's quiet in the village. No missed calls or messages either."

Unsurprising. The only people who ever contacted me were my family and my boss. I'd had a phone back in school, but I got rid of it after graduating college. I had few friends to start with, and I stopped reaching out completely when I became a shut-in. Since then, I only really spoke with my family. I'd only talk to my friends if they initiated contact, until even the one friend who stuck with me for years eventually stopped trying.

I couldn't bring back the past. I knew that better than anyone. Once I closed off my heart, life became too difficult, and I lived locked away in a cage of my own making.

I left the store, shivering as the cold winter air hit me at full force. My breath came out in small puffs of white mist.

"I'm just a walking bundle of regret."

When had I last seen my friend? I'd known her since child-hood; we grew up next door to each other. She was in my very oldest memories. We'd practically been together since birth, attending the same schools, even the same university. My chest felt heavy as I thought about her.

"I ran away. From work, from my friends, from my family. From my memories, and from reality."

I looked up at the night sky as I walked home. The houses and streetlights were thin along this road, leaving the stars and moon clearly visible.

"We went to see some falling stars when we were in school..."

During the best days of my life, she was always there with me.

I wonder what she's doing now?

I didn't feel like going straight home, so I took a roundabout route. When I reached my house, I noticed a woman in a suit standing outside our neighbor's place. Her left foot was in a cast, and she was on crutches. She was struggling to get her key out.

"Seika..."

Tsumabuki Seika, my childhood friend. Her long dark brown hair was tied back, and she wore a pair of frameless glasses. For a second, I stood in awe at the sight of her. Then she turned around at the sound of my voice, and her eyes widened.

How long had it been?

Seika's face was feminine, with soft, rounded eyes. Like me, she was in her thirties but looked like late twenties at most.

"Yoshi..."

I wondered what I looked like to her, standing there in my coveralls. We always said we'd get jobs at the same place, but I hadn't worn a suit in years. My only one was currently in my closet collecting dust.

"It's been a while. And, uh, please don't call me Yoshi. I'm not a dinosaur."

I was surprised at myself, speaking to her so easily. So much time had passed, but a few years of no contact was nothing in the face of more than two decades of friendship. Even if we didn't speak, I saw Seika just a few weeks ago. As in, on days I got up early enough, I sometimes watched her head out for work from my bedroom window. I wasn't sure how long it had been since she'd seen me, though. Probably years.

"Is your foot okay?"

"Oh, yeah. I was in an accident and went to the hospital, but it's just a fracture. I'm getting rides to work with a coworker, so it's all good."

The tinge of relief in her voice and the way she self-consciously held a hand up to her cheek made memories rush back to me. I couldn't help but smile.

"Glad it's nothing worse than that."

Now that she was here, I realized there was a ton of stuff I wanted to talk about, but it was the middle of the night and freezing. And Seika was injured. I couldn't justify keeping her out here. I only called out to her on a whim; I didn't actually have anything important to say.

"See you around."

"Wait a second. Why don't you come in? I mean, it's just me and Granny anyway." Sadness colored her voice. Seika's parents passed away a few years ago, and she had been living here with her grandmother ever since.

"I'll pass. I don't wanna wake up Okiku-baachan."

Also...we would be a grown man and woman together in the middle of the night, even if I did know her from childhood.

"Oh, right..." Seika looked down at the ground with a small nod.

I remembered that habit of hers. It meant she had given up trying to convince me. She was always like this. The moment her ideas got shot down, she would instantly retreat out of respect for others.

"Let's chat again soon. I'm sure Mom would love to talk to you, too. Why don't you come over with Okiku-baachan some time?"

"What? Are you serious?" Seika's eyes widened in surprise.

This was the first time in years that I ever reached out to her.

"Course. You can come by whenever I'm not at work."

I knew my lack of employment was something she used to worry about, so I thought I should let her know I found something now. Though she'd probably already worked it out from my coveralls.

"Oh yeah, I heard you got a job. Obaasan and Sayuki-chan told me. They said you're working really hard." Seika looked into my eyes, a tender smile on her face.

I wasn't aware she still spoke to my family. Unlike me, Seika got a job right out of college and now worked for a large corporation. Doubtless she made way more money than me, but there was no pity or scorn in her voice. She seemed genuinely happy for me. Only a few weeks ago, I would have been too cynical to take her words at face value.

Seika was the same as ever. Even if age had changed her features a little, her heart remained kind. Unlike mine.

"Oh, and the fruit and meat your family shared with us was delicious."

"I'm glad you liked it."

I vaguely remembered Mom asking if she could share it with the neighbors. I probably just shrugged. I was about to turn around and go home, before realizing I shouldn't just leave her struggling with her keys. I walked over and held her shoulders so she wouldn't fall, taking the key from her and opening the door.

"See you later."

"Th-thanks. I'll come visit soon, okay?"

"Looking forward to it."

I closed the door for her once she was inside and made my way home.

The moment I was through the door, I let out a huge sigh and slumped down against it. I barely said anything to her at all, yet I was exhausted. Both Seika and I knew how well we got on with each other. People used to say we were basically married, even back then. We were more than friends but never quite made it to lovers. My plan was to confess to her once we graduated and I found a good job.

That never happened. Seika found work straight away, but I never got anywhere, becoming more and more desperate by the day. I couldn't face confessing to her when she had a better job than me, so I kept aiming for places just as good as hers or better. I failed every single time. She was always there to cheer me on, but even that started to irritate me, so I distanced myself from her. The only word for it was...pathetic.

"She's been waiting and thinking about me this whole time... Wait, who am I kidding? She probably stopped caring ages ago."

My world had frozen, but society moved on without me. Even if Seika *was* devoted enough to wait for me to come to my senses, she was a lovely woman. The world kept turning, and I'm sure she'd met men ten times more impressive than me by now. She might have fallen in love with one of them, too, and I had no right to complain. Seika wasn't married yet, but she was most likely dating someone. Maybe even the person giving her rides to work. I knew we couldn't go back to the way things used to be, but perhaps she would be willing to be friends...

I felt my chest swell up painfully with regret after regret. I wanted to punch myself in the face.

THE NPCs IN THIS VILLAGE SIM GAME MUST BE REAL! ↵

chapter 02
Everybody's Journey and My Forgetfulness

THREE DAYS HAD PASSED since Murus joined the village. I hadn't seen Seika since we spoke outside her house, but if she was going to come over, it would probably be on the weekend. Nothing was happening in real life, and the game world was peaceful, too, especially compared to a few days earlier. Murus was still far from her old self, but she was smiling more and more, especially when she spent time with Carol. I just hoped their bond could help heal Murus's wounds. Her existence was a great help to the village, but more than that, I wished for her happiness and the happiness of all my villagers. As their God, that was all I wanted.

Murus told the others she was an elf, and they accepted it without fuss. Some of them might have worked it out already, what with her living in the forest, being a physician, using plant magic, and practicing archery. Carol was particularly impressed, her eyes lighting up when Murus told them. She must have known elves from a picture book or something. Murus seemed surprised but relieved at their reaction, and soon she was smiling, too.

I'd been worried they wouldn't accept her, but I wasn't about to let any of them know that.

I didn't have work today, so I planned to just to chill and keep an eye on the village, when after breakfast, Murus came out with something unexpected.

"Would you like to come to my village today?"

What? Her village was destroyed, right? She said so herself. What was the point of going there? Unless...

"Most of the buildings have been destroyed, but there should be some materials left. Some necessities that are still usable, and some food, too."

Right, that made sense. Extra supplies were always welcome.

"I'm sure those things would be useful, but are you really okay with that?" Rodice asked.

"Of course. Tools are useless without a master. Plus, you avenged my village. The inhabitants would be glad to know their things are in your hands."

If Murus had no objections, then neither did I. The villagers seemed to feel the same way. There was just one problem.

"I wanna go, too! Lemme go!"

"Now, Carol, you mustn't be selfish. I've told you many times how dangerous the forest is." Rodice pleaded with his daughter, who was flailing around desperately on the floor.

Carol was usually very sensible, so watching her throw a tantrum was strange. Though I guess it was stranger *not* to see a kid her age occasionally act out.

"What's wrong? You're not usually like this."

"'Cause it's not fair! Chem always gets to go everywhere, and I always have to stay here! Chem can't even fight or anything, just like me! So why can't I go, too?" Carol wailed.

Chem stumbled backwards, clutching at her chest.

Looks like she hit a nerve...

Sure, Chem wasn't able to help defeat the one-eyed red goblin, but without her the villagers would not have received a proper burial. I was glad she was there, but Chem herself seemed self-conscious about her shoddy combat skills.

Carol's parents tried to calm her down, but she was being particularly stubborn today.

"She's always stuck in this dark cave or inside the fence. I'm not surprised she's sick of it. She's just a kid, after all," Gams said.

I was surprised. Gams was usually the one most determined to keep everyone out of danger.

"Gams! Can I come, too?"

"No, you can't! Gams, it's far too dangerous! I cannot agree with this!" Chem protested.

Gams placed a pacifying hand on each of their heads.

"Listen, you two. We already wiped out the enemies that attacked Murus's village. The woods around there should be tranquil for now. Besides, we can't just leave Carol here by herself. Carol, you've gotta promise to do everything we say, no matter what. D'you think you can handle it?"

"I sure can!" Carol nodded furiously.

Gams leaned forward to whisper in his sister's ear. "Rodice and Lyra'll come too if Carol does, and being cooped up in the cave all the time isn't good for them, either. It's a good idea all around."

Gams was even more compassionate toward the other villagers than I was. I owed him a lot for taking care of them. Murus told us she had already buried all of her dead, so there would be no danger of my characters coming across any corpses.

I knew more than anyone how mentally damaging it was to stay holed up in a cramped room for weeks on end. Even in Japan—a relatively safe country—my thoughts spiraled. I could only imagine how anxious you would be with danger lurking right outside your front door. Staying active and sane was important.

"Let us travel by horse," Murus suggested. "We can find a cart in the village to transport whatever we find back here."

Was there even a usable cart? They might get more out of this trip than I thought! My village had a cart, too, but it had been partially destroyed during the opening cutscene. A usable vehicle would make transporting goods or fleeing—should it come to that—much easier. Even Lyra and Rodice, who were hesitant about the trip, grew more interested when Murus mentioned the cart.

My villagers kept two horses that they let outside within the fence to graze during the day and brought back into the shelter of the cave at night. Sometimes, Gams and Murus took them out hunting or gathering. As much as I didn't like to think about it, I knew the villagers planned to eat the horses eventually. But with a wagon to pull, those creatures' futures might be brighter.

"Looks like they won't be sending me any horse meat, then... Oh well."

The horses had been with us from the beginning, and I'd had a while to get to know them. They even had names, courtesy of Carol.

"Parochoot and Peperopont! You guys get to come, too!" Carol beamed as she stroked the two creatures.

Sorry, Carol, I know you're just a kid, but those names are awful...

They sounded to me like a couple of words she just made up on the spot.

My villagers prepared and set off on their first journey as a full group in a long while. Lyra and Carol rode the horses, while the other four went on foot. The journey through the forest and over the river would have been a quick one, but the wooden bridge was broken, rendering that route impassable. They were forced to take a detour, following the bank and fording downriver.

I kept watch from above as they walked. They were traveling with non-combatants, and it didn't hurt to be cautious. Since Murus was officially a villager now, I could also see everywhere she'd been on the map. Part of my daily routine was scrolling across the now-visible Forbidden Forest, checking out the places Gams and the others had never been. The newly visible area was more than ten times what I could see before. Still, I couldn't see the entire forest.

"I wonder just how far the map goes."

The reduced fog of war let me notice a couple of things. The first was that Murus had never left the forest. She'd been right up to the border, but everything beyond was still hidden. Most of the area around her village was now visible, but there were still certain areas covered in darkness she must have avoided. Those places were likely dangerous. Maybe the monsters there were powerful, or maybe there was some other reason, but we should keep our distance.

Most of the north side of the forest was hidden, whereas the entirety of the south was visible. The Forbidden Forest seemed to grow more dangerous the farther north you went. This was the direction my villagers fled from, too.

Unfortunately, none of the newly revealed parts of the map seemed to contain any settlements, aside from Murus's desolate village. Tons of stuff to look at, but I tried to keep my attention on the cave and the surrounding areas. Initially, I planned to explore the new spaces once my villagers were asleep, but without any light, the forest was pitch-black. I couldn't see a thing.

While I was wrapped up in my thoughts, my villagers made steady progress.

"Yay! Outside!" Carol cheered as she waved a stick around atop her horse.

Gams led her horse by the reins. Carol had dubbed him her knight, and he appeared to be enjoying the role.

"How's the horse, my princess?" he asked.

Wow! He's playing along!

"It's very comfortable! You may stand closer to me!"

Carol played a better princess than I expected, too. Chem was looking at them with a smile that veered toward a scowl.

"She'd be the perfect holy woman, if only she didn't fawn over her brother like that," I mumbled.

As a brother myself, I appreciated a good brother-sister relationship, but Chem took it a little too far for my taste. It would take hell freezing over for Sayuki to ever get to *this* level.

The odd monster appeared on the map, but none of them were close enough to notice or attack my villagers. At this pace, they would reach Murus's village within the next five minutes. I zoomed in close, hiding the rest of the map from view. If I spent the entire time focused on their surroundings, I'd miss a bunch of their interactions. Multitasking was tougher than I thought.

I clicked over to check on Murus's village at the end of their path, just to make sure there weren't any monsters lurking or anything that I didn't want Carol to see. She was far less sheltered than kids her age in Japan, but as an adult, I still wanted to protect her as much as I could.

"This is a pretty big village. They must've had a hundred people or so."

I counted about thirty destroyed houses. Most of them were razed down to their foundations, but a few buildings clung on to their structural integrity. The wooden dwellings were done for, but the stone ones came through with huge craters in their walls and roofs. If those were patched up, they'd be livable.

I wondered briefly if my villagers could move here but quickly dismissed it. The city walls were completely decimated, and even if my people repaired them, there was no telling if they would survive the next Day of Corruption. The place was too large to defend with just six people. If they were going to live here, I'd want thirty, if not fifty, inhabitants at least. I tabled that idea and focused.

"This looks like somewhere we could find food."

I clicked on one of the least damaged houses, and the game switched at once to an interior view. I was surprised; I hadn't been able to see inside the green goblins' huts. Maybe it was to shield my eyes from the horrors within.

Inside, the house was pretty wrecked. I checked the shelves, looking in pots that might contain food, but they were completely empty. I was about to move from the kitchen into one of the other rooms when the door opened. A stocky man stood at the head of a group of burly fighters, all carrying weapons.

chapter 03

The Forgotten Miracle and My Confusion

I NEVER EXPECTED to find anyone here, and I nearly leapt to my feet in surprise. Slowly, I sat back in my seat. Fortunately, my villagers weren't here yet. I had time to handle this.

First, I took a good look at this group of men. I thought they might be survivors from Murus's village, but their appearance swiftly told me otherwise. Their ears were rounded at the top and, to say it mildly, they weren't exactly stunning beauties. The man in front was plump and middle-aged, and though all of them were armed, he wore travelers' clothes—a thick coat and boots made of leather, simple yet well made.

The man frowned at the desolation surrounding him. He was accompanied by two men in leather armor who reminded me of Gams, as well as a woman in light clothes, armed with a short sword and a bow. A small, cloaked figure lurked behind them, a hood pulled low over their face, leaving me with no clue as to their identity, but the large staff they carried suggested they might be a sorcerer.

"Apart from that guy in the front, these look like your typical fantasy adventurers. Wonder if they're hunters or something."

It always struck me as weird that "adventurer" was considered a profession in fantasy settings. Most of their money seemed to come from taking requests to slay monsters and then selling their parts afterwards. In this world, "hunter" was probably the better term. Chem and Gams would fall under that category, too.

No matter the setting, adventurers always struck me as underpaid for the risk they took on. Factoring in the danger, one dead monster should provide enough to live on comfortably for at least a month. Without a huge financial incentive, it made no sense why anyone would want to become an adventurer in the first place, and yet it seemed like a common profession.

Anyway, that wasn't important right now. I had to figure out who this group was. I tried clicking on them, but all I got was "???" Totally unhelpful. I zoomed in close to try to see what they were saying. Their mouths were moving, but there were no text boxes.

"Should've seen that coming."

I'd been curious about when text boxes showed up and when they didn't, and recently I'd investigated it. From what I could tell, I could see conversations happening within a certain distance of the holy book. When the group set out to the goblin's territory, their entire conversation was logged, but I got nothing from Rodice's family back at the cave. Other things had distance restrictions, too. At the goblin's camp, I controlled the tiny doll Carol carved, but I couldn't activate the golem back at the cave. In other words, everything I could do in the game revolved around that book.

I could only perform miracles in its vicinity. That was important information to remember to avoid fatal mistakes. Actually, that was one of the reasons I wanted Rodice's family to come to the village. I couldn't rely on using the golem to protect them if they stayed in the cave.

"Ugh, I'm getting distracted again!"

Who were these people? Likely just a group of hunters who happened to stumble on the village at the same time as us. The middle-aged guy looked weak, but he very well might be trained in martial arts. Characters in manga and light novels often looked normal but hid extraordinary talents. It seemed like he'd hired this group of hunters, and they were following his orders.

The woman took the lead, checking each house before returning and letting the others know it was safe to go inside. One of the armed men always remained beside the leader.

"Maybe a merchant and his guard?"

A reasonable guess, considering the leader's huge rucksack. The group probably just detoured here when they saw the village had been destroyed. I zoomed right into that middle-aged man and found he had quite a friendly face. He even put his hands together and prayed respectfully before he entered each house.

I'd be worried it was an act if he knew he was being watched, but he didn't. I assumed this was his true nature.

"Should I send a prophecy to let my guys know they aren't alone? Maybe not, since that will use up my shot if there's a real crisis." I'd be typing up a prophecy this second if I really thought these strangers were bad news.

Maybe I should prepare one just in case...

Neither group knew of the other's existence, but my villagers were fast approaching them.

"This is driving me nuts!"

I hoped my group would notice first. I kept watching, almost forgetting to breathe.

"This is the village I used to live in," Murus said as they reached the entrance. "Would you mind waiting here for a second while I go on ahead?"

Even if there weren't any dead bodies or monsters left, Murus was conscious that my villagers had witnessed this kind of destruction before and didn't want them to see it again.

"Don't worry about us," Rodice said. "Carol might be a little upset, but we have to face this eventually."

"That's right. Who's to say we won't wake up tomorrow to something even worse?" added Lyra.

The world on the other side of the screen was a totally different place from the haven of Japan. Naturally, they were protective of their children, but in such a dangerous place they could only do so much. If they didn't desensitize Carol to this, she might freeze when it really mattered and get herself killed.

"I'm super strong! You don't hafta worry!" Carol reassured them, though her tiny fists were trembling.

Gams picked up on her fear right away and took her hand. Carol gave a small smile of relief. I took a curious glance at Chem, but she appeared to recognize any jealousy right now would be childish. She just smiled gently, and if her fingers were digging hard into her holy book, well, I could pretend I didn't notice.

I hovered over the keyboard as my villagers entered the destroyed settlement. We were in the southern section, while the mysterious group was in the northeast. The two groups would converge in the town center; it wouldn't be long before they spotted each other.

"Chem! Get behind that house, now. Murus! Over here!"

"Someone's there. It might be monsters or looters. Either way, we cannot allow them to escape."

Gams pulled out his swords as Murus prepared her bow. Chem was silent as she led the horses and Rodice's family behind the ruins of a house. The other group had noticed us as well, sending the woman and one of the armed men out ahead. The other three followed at a distance. With no idea how this would end, my palm grew sweaty where I held it above the mouse.

"What business have you here...Dordold?!" Murus lowered her bow.

"Murus! You're safe! Everyone, sheath your weapons!"

The two guards did as their leader ordered, and Gams put away his swords. "Dordold" went to Murus and took her warmly by the hand.

"I was terrified when I found the village in this state! I'm just so glad to see you're all right!" Dordold sighed, wiping the tears from his eyes.

I was relieved I'd been right—he didn't seem like a bad person at all.

"I'm all right, yes, but I'm afraid everyone else wasn't so lucky. Do not fear, my friends. This is Dordold. He is a traveling merchant who passed through our village to sell his wares from time to time. I have full faith in him, as did my people."

Chem and the others reappeared from behind the ruins. I was right about him being a merchant, too. Wow, two in one day. Pretty good, with my track record. What's more, elves held this man in high esteem, which was saying something, considering their general distrust of humans. Perhaps it was Dordold's influence that made Murus hesitant to treat my villagers as enemies when they first met.

Besides, a merchant was just what we needed. My villagers could sell monster hides and bones to him, and maybe even some of the ore from the cave. Surely this merchant had his own stock, and my villagers could purchase things to help them through the winter. Rodice had already started haggling.

"Guess I don't need this prophecy anymore."

I quickly deleted the message I'd prepared earlier. I didn't want to send it by accident and make stuff awkward. Dordold genuinely seemed like a nice guy, if a little weepy. He was still dabbing at his eyes with a handkerchief and glancing at Murus as if to make sure she was really there.

"It is a pleasure to meet you all. I will be happy to buy whatever you wish to sell. Once you have finished your business here, could I accompany you back to your cave?"

"Of course! You would be helping us out a great deal," Rodice said. As a fellow merchant, it seemed he'd taken a liking to Dordold. I decided to leave the bartering up to him, too.

And so, my villagers set to work gathering what they could.

With Murus's permission, they searched for both necessities and valuables that Dordold might be willing to buy. Most of the town's carts were damaged beyond repair, but my villagers dismantled and gathered the usable parts and managed to put them together into one fully functional cart to take home with them.

"I'm glad everything worked out. I didn't even activate any events or anything!" Suddenly, I remembered something. "Wait..."

When Murus joined my village, I *did* activate a miracle: "Spawn a traveling merchant." So Dordold's appearance was totally my doing! That was three days ago; it seemed some miracles weren't instantaneous. Oh well. At least I learned something new.

After a few hours, my villagers wrapped up their scavenging.

Chem prayed in front of the graves of the deceased. "Rest in peace."

Carol laid down some flowers on the graves that she'd picked with Dordold's guards. I watched everyone praying and decided to do my bit by performing another miracle. I activated the blue skies so that a single ray of light beamed down over the graves. The particles of dust in the air sparkled, as though I were calling the dead up to heaven.

"Maybe this is kinda over the top, but it sure is pretty..."

Murus watched the graves of her friends bathed in sunlight, tears falling from her eyes.

chapter 04
Unprejudiced People and My Lack of Naming Sense

MY VILLAGERS MADE THEIR WAY home in their expanded group, the two wagons trundling carefully down the wild forest path. One was the cart put together in Murus's village, and one was Dordold's, hidden among the trees. The group numbered eleven in total: the three of Rodice's family, Chem and Gams, Murus, Dordold, and his four hunters. Though there were barely any salvageable materials in the village, the tableware, preserved goods, salt, and spices were more than enough to keep everyone happy. But the vegetable seeds they picked up were what really excited me. They wouldn't be able to grow anything over the winter, but I couldn't wait for spring.

With so many people in their group, I didn't need to worry about their safety. I got up from the computer and headed downstairs.

After a quick trip to the bathroom, I grabbed some of yesterday's leftover meat and some of the village fruit from the fridge. I piled my plate high to feed my lizard while I was at it.

"You hungry? I got you some—Wow, that was quick..."

The lizard sat down next to the plate, already nibbling at the fruit. This guy was way too good at letting itself out whenever it felt like it. I glanced at the tank. The top was askew. I was impressed how smart this lizard was, but *how* exactly was it doing this? None of the sand or the fallen-tree decorations inside the tank were high enough for it to climb up to the top.

"How did you get outta there?"

Ignoring my question and finishing off the fruit, the lizard went for some of the plain meat this time, tearing off large chunks and chewing loudly.

"You eat meat, too, huh? You're an omnivore?"

It ignored me again, continuing to eat. I assumed meat wouldn't hurt it, since it tore into it so cheerfully, but I made a mental note to double-check with Sayuki later.

My lizard was eating and growing at a good pace. It was around the size of a small plushie now, a big increase in just a few days. I just hoped it wasn't planning to grow as long as one of those massive snakes. This current size was perfect.

"Oh, right. I came up with some names for you. Lemme know which one you want. My first idea was Lizardosaurus, 'cause you look like a dragon."

The lizard stared at me, dropping its meat. It looked horrified, too horrified to even shake its head. While telling myself it was just coincidence, I accepted that it didn't like "Lizardosaurus."

"What about this then? 'Destiny.' It's like another word for 'fate.' Perfect, right?"

Picking up the meat again, the lizard nodded. I knew there was no way it really understood me, but I took it as a "yes" anyway. Excellent. "Destiny" was a perfect fit for the God of Fate's pet. The two of us ate our fruit together, Destiny finishing up before me. It turned to stare at the computer. I followed Destiny's gaze to find my villagers arriving back at their cave.

I nearly forgot about them!

Not that I had anything to do but watch right now. Rodice was in charge of buying and selling; I was glad to have him in the village. This would be a good chance for him to show his daughter the ropes before she ran off to be Gams's housewife. As far as I was concerned, it would be good for her.

"I see. This is where you're living. Yes...easy to guard and well sheltered. You have a skilled archer and a proficient hunter. A physician and a healer. Not to mention an adorable little girl and her beautiful and competent mother. It's the perfect mix of people!"

Dordold knew how to pay a compliment. He also agreed to buy our monster parts for more than their market value. Rodice pointed it out, not wanting him to make a mistake.

"Please allow me to add a little extra. You are blessed by the God of Fate, after all. I'm sure you have a prosperous future. May He continue to watch over you."

I decided that I liked Dordold as a merchant as much as I liked him as a person. My villagers showed him some of their cave ore, but it wasn't worth that much for how heavy it was. He promised to come back for it another time.

"I'm always happy to buy goods for money, but next time perhaps we could barter?" Dordold said.

"That works for us," Rodice agreed. "I have one more favor to ask, if you wouldn't mind. As you can see, there are only a few of us here. If you ever come across somebody looking for a new home, could you let them know we'd welcome them?"

I almost sent a prophecy adding "I'll throw in my divine protection for free!" but managed to restrain myself.

"People looking for a home," Dordold murmured. "Yes, many places have seen their fair share of trouble lately. You cannot go far without news of another village destroyed by monsters. Word is that they are growing more violent, and different species are joining together to make coordinated attacks. I am sure there are many refugees out there."

My village wasn't the only one, then. Monsters were acting strangely and attacking settlements all over this world.

"However, the Forbidden Forest is, quite frankly, a dangerous place to live. If I may be so bold, why don't you think about moving somewhere else?"

What a proposal. I was worried I might get a "game over" if my villagers moved away from the forest. If they just joined a settlement somewhere, wouldn't that defeat the whole purpose of a village-building sim? But if that meant they could be safe and happy, it wouldn't be so much "game over" as *winning* the game. I would hate to give up, but I wanted to prioritize my villagers' happiness. If staying in this cave meant they were all going to die one day, then of course I'd choose to prevent that.

Whatever my villagers decided, I would accept. No interfering with any prophecies. I watched them anxiously, preparing for the worst.

"Thank you, but I want to remain here. Reckless, maybe, seeing as I have my family to think about, but this is where the God of Fate led us. I feel as though we owe it to Him to stay here."

"Every good wife must support her husband's decisions. The family must stick together."

"Yeah! I wanna live with Mommy and Daddy and Gams and Murus!"

Rodice's family all voiced their desire to stay. Carol excluding Chem like that was rude, but whatever. I ignored Chem's rictus smile at the little girl's back.

"This is where the Lord gives us His blessings. I intend to live the rest of my life under His watchful eye."

"I'll do my utmost to keep everyone safe."

Chem and Gams added their voices.

"I have only ever known the forest, and this is where I feel at home. I do not want to leave my fallen villagers either," Murus said.

Every last one of them wanted to stay. They were counting on me to look after them. I had to live up to those hopes.

I'm gonna make them the best damn village I can!

This was supposed to be a village-building sim, but so far it felt more like a survival game, the way my villagers were just roughing it in a cave. The only building they'd done so far was putting a bunch of logs together to make that watchtower and the fence. The forest had no shortage of trees. I figured I should encourage them to build a small hut or something soon. If we gained more villagers, the few rooms in the cave wouldn't be enough.

"I understand. I won't judge where you call home. Come to think of it, I might know a group who'd happily live in a place like this. They were chased out of their previous home, you see."

As an experienced merchant, I trusted Dordold to be a good judge of character. Better than me, at least, considering I'd just spent a decade not talking to anyone.

"Thank you."

"Just leave it to me, Rodice. I shall try to return here within the next few weeks. If there's anything you need, let me know before I leave, and I can get it for you."

Rodice mentioned they could do with some more clothes and underwear. When they left their village, they didn't have time to pack garments and had therefore been wearing the same outfits ever since. It was only recently that they tanned some animal pelts and made gowns for the female villagers to wear while they slept.

Their conversation finished, Dordold and his guards left on a cart and horse. Carol continued to wave even long after they were out of sight.

"Whew. They're all set for winter now. Sounds like we'll get some new people, too."

They'd dealt with a ton of my worries today. The opportunity to salvage materials from Murus's village had to be part of the bonus event. I'd have to thank Sayuki for accidentally activating that when she was at my computer.

I glanced at the window to see it was already dark out. The winter nights were quickly growing shorter. I turned on my phone to check if anything came in while I was focusing on my game and found a message from Sayuki.

I'm gonna be home late today. If you're not busy, could you pick me up from the bus stop? I'll call you when I'm close.

I agreed without a second thought. I knew she was worried about that stalker, and I decided I would do whatever I could to help her feel safe. That's what brothers were for, after all. Besides, walking her back from the bus stop wasn't that big an ask.

"I'll send today's prophecy real quick before I forget."

I checked the whole map before writing it, just in case there was danger lurking. After what happened today, I wanted them to be sure I was watching over them. I wrote a small message of prayer for Murus's villagers.

"I welcome our new villager with open arms, and I pray those you left behind find peace in the next life. May the farewells and meetings you had today soothe your aching heart."

I always made sure my prophecies weren't too wordy, especially when I didn't have anything important to say. After reading my message, my villagers closed their eyes and put their hands together in prayer. I felt like I wasn't quite able to say the right words, but this was the best I could do.

"Yoshio! Dinner!" Mom called, summoning me to the table.

Dad was also working late, so dinner tonight was just me and her. When we were done, I took my bath and settled down in my futon...which was when I remembered.

"Wait...I'm supposed to go pick up Sayuki!"

That was close. I was glad I hadn't fallen asleep—she would've killed me. No word from her yet, but I wanted to do some shopping anyway. I headed out early, pulling on a warm hooded jacket and a big backpack to carry my purchases. Even though I left the house most days now, I still wasn't used to how cold it got. My ears were already stinging in the brisk air. I pulled my hood up and hurried to the store.

The convenience store lit up the night like an oasis in the dark. I watched it from a distance as I made my way down the long, sloping path past the shrine. We were miles from the nearest city out here in the countryside, and that convenience store was the only one around, rendering it an important spot. Its bright lights made for a good landmark in the middle of the night. A gas station stood opposite it, but it was a small, family-run business and closed at 9 p.m. I mentioned that to some of my online friends, and they thought it was hilarious. In the city, most gas stations apparently had self-service and were open twenty-four hours a day.

It had been a while since I last chatted with my online friends. I wondered how they were doing. I wished I was allowed to tell them about *The Village of Fate*.

Before I knew it, I was at the convenience store. Sayuki still hadn't messaged me and the last bus wasn't due for a while, so I headed into the store to kill time. On the way in, I passed a man in a suit. I stopped. His back was slightly hunched, and he was smirking. A freezing chill raced up my spine and spread through my entire body.

I recognized that face. He'd grown taller—as tall as me—but there was no mistaking those features.

"It can't be..."

I would never forget that face. The face of that kid in Sayuki's class. The kid who stabbed me.

Sayuki leaned over me, sobbing hysterically. I lay on the ground, blood spilling from my stomach. That kid glared madly, shouting something.

The pain was so vivid, even now. My chest tightened, and I struggled to breathe. He was found guilty of assault and sent to an institute for young offenders, and released a few years later. I knew that. I just didn't know he was still in town. Although, it made sense—he was born and raised here. But why was he loitering around the bus stop right when my sister was expected back?

Attempting to prevent myself from freaking out, I went over to the magazine rack by the window and grabbed one at random, all the while keeping an eye on that man through the glass. He walked across a parking lot beside the store, leaned against the wall, and began to text on his phone, drinking a canned coffee. He kept looking up towards the bus stop. I was confident he was too engrossed in his phone to recognize me with my hood up when I walked past. He didn't seem to know he was being watched, either.

The way he was behaving...he had to be the stalker Sayuki was afraid of. I already guessed it might have been the same guy, but I was desperately hoping it wasn't true.

What do I do now?

Sayuki and I already spoke with the police about the suspicious figure we'd seen, but they said they couldn't do anything if a crime hadn't been committed. They did say they would increase patrols, but I only saw policemen out twice around our house. This time of year must be busy for them.

"What *should* I do, as her brother?"

I was courting danger, but anything was better than this guy jumping my sister when she got off the bus. Acting before she arrived might be my best option. I tried phoning her and sending a text, but she didn't respond.

How much time 'til her bus comes in?

I paid for the magazine I picked up and left the store. Then, I approached the man smirking at his phone.

chapter 05 The Stalker and My Actions

T HE MAN WAS faced away from me. The bus wasn't here yet, and he wasn't trying to hide. I began to worry that I'd jumped to the wrong conclusion. Maybe he was here for something else— I looked around, searching for any clues. The odd car passed by, a minivan sat parked in front of the convenience store, and two young men stood on the street, chatting and laughing. They were close enough to hear me if I shouted for help. They looked self-absorbed and unlikely to help a stranger, but Yamamoto-san taught me not to judge people by their appearances. If I was in danger, I'd make sure everyone knew it. The stalker wouldn't do anything in front of witnesses. I hoped.

He was arrested once already, shouldn't that be enough to deter him from stalking in the future? Apparently not. But he'd at least want to avoid getting in trouble with the law, right?

He was an adult now, too. Even if he didn't seriously injure me, he'd be sent to prison for assault.

Should I call the cops?

And tell them what? "I found the guy who used to stalk my sister. Please come arrest him"?

He was already under a restraining order, but he could just claim he was here by coincidence. I decided to wait and see. I'd only call the police if he was clearly actually stalking her again.

But what if he did something horrific before I could stop him? I'd regret not acting sooner for the rest of my life. Then again, if he *was* innocent, calling the cops would just piss him off—maybe even enough to provoke him. And if I called the police right now, would they even make it in time? And if they stopped him acting now, he could just come back later, right? I wanted to make sure he wouldn't come near Sayuki ever again.

Like I said, I didn't think he would attack me, but I couldn't be sure. The logical part of my brain was calm, but I unconsciously traced a hand across my scar. My mind raced as I moved closer and closer.

God, what should I say to him? Should I try to be casual?

"Sup! Remember me? You stabbed me, like, ten years ago. Ah ha ha! Good times!"

No way, that was absolutely the quickest way to provoke him. *Maybe I should pretend I only realized who he was as I walked by?* I wasn't sure. If I made it obvious that I knew who he was and what he was doing here, maybe that would stop him from doing anything stupid.

My thoughts ran in dizzy circles. I kept repeating to myself that he might not be here for any nefarious purpose at all. I just needed to know how he viewed everything that had happened.

Then I'd know if he was worth worrying about in the first place. If things looked dicey, I could run and get help. Cowardly, maybe, but I had to put my own safety first here.

The man was still looking at his phone. He hadn't seen me yet.

I didn't want to get too close, so I stopped a few meters away from him and called out casually. "Huh? Is that you, Yoshinaga-kun?"

He spun around to face me with obvious shock. He frowned, dubious. From this close there was no doubt. He was absolutely Sayuki's old stalker, Yoshinaga.

"Um, sorry, but...who are you?"

What? You don't remember the face of the guy you stabbed?

His tone was calm. Polite, even. But suspicion crowded his gaze.

"You don't remember that whole thing with my sister?" I lowered my hood and took a step forward into the light of the streetlamp.

I didn't miss the way his expression changed.

"Oh...are you Sayuki-san's brother?"

Now he remembered me. I could see where this might be going.

"Yup. Haven't seen you around in while."

I wasn't about to ask him how he'd been. He could very well blame me for his time spent locked up in that institution. Yoshinaga's lawyer told me he cried about how sorry he was and kept saying "Sorry, Sayuki!" Apparently my name never came up. I remembered his glare after he stabbed me, like I was nothing but a nuisance. I'd never forget that look as long as I lived. He sent me a letter afterward about how "sorry" he was, but there was no real feeling in it.

"I caused you guys a lot of trouble..." Yoshinaga bowed deeply.

It was the first time he ever apologized directly to me, but the gesture felt empty. I always wondered how he might act if we happened to meet each other again—if he regretted his actions—but I wasn't naive enough to take him at face value.

"It's in the past now. I'm sorry for the stuff I said to you, too. I should've thought before opening my mouth."

I gave a level response and waited to see how he'd take it. There was a definite tension in the air. I felt like a single slipup might break things down completely.

"No, what I did was unforgivable. Not only stalking Sayuki-san but hurting you, as well."

Maybe he was *actually* trying to show some remorse and turn his life around. His speech was perfectly polite, his words carefully chosen.

"You've already been through your punishment. Please, raise your head."

I wanted to add "as long as you're not thinking of hurting my sister," but I didn't want to push it. I was surprised at how well I was taking this. I could still feel that knife sinking into my stomach, the blood pouring out of me. That absolute terror. I still dreamed about it, shocking awake so hard I nearly fell out of bed.

If this were a TV drama, maybe I'd be able to forgive him and hug it out. But this was real life, and I wasn't going to forget. Just being around him made me so anxious my palms were sweating.

"You know, I never expected to meet you here at this time of night," I said.

"This is the only twenty-four-hour store in town. I'm just here on my way back from work."

Perfectly reasonable. This *was* the only convenience store around. Maybe this really was just a coincidence. Could Sayuki's current stalker be someone else entirely?

"You must be working hard if you're finishing this late."

"Yeah, it's rough!"

I chose my words carefully. If I didn't know any better, he'd come off like a normal, driven young man. A stranger asked to choose which one of us was a stalker would most likely pick the guy who spent the last ten years holed up in his room.

"Sorry for talking to you out of the blue. But I'd...really appreciate it if you could avoid my sister, going forward."

"Of course. My feelings were out of control back then. I haven't gone near her once since I got released. I've never even seen her around." He looked me straight in the eye as he said this.

"Thanks, that makes me feel better. D'you mind if I ask you something?"

"Of course. Anything." Yoshinaga straightened up, ready to hear my request.

"Why are you still stalking her?"

"What?"

I walked closer, lowering my voice. "I know you're still following her."

"Wh-what are you talking about?"

"Don't forget about the restraining order. I bumped into you around here before, remember? You saw me and then ran away. Why?"

I wasn't asking, I was *telling*. Sayuki said I tended to look away when I was lying. I wasn't going to look away now, no matter how scared I was.

He returned my gaze evenly.

Last time, I didn't see the stalker's face. I needed to know for sure whether it was Yoshinaga or not. If it wasn't, I could just apologize to him and let him go. Keeping Sayuki safe was worth the embarrassment of a false accusation.

I narrowed my eyes, feigning confidence I didn't feel. The silence seemed to last forever.

"Huh. Guess you caught me. I'll drop the act, then. I was gettin' sick of it anyway."

No way...

Yoshinaga scratched casually at the back of his neck. "Y'know, the two of us aren't so different. I was locked away, too."

He grinned at me. Anger sparked in my chest as he struck at my insecurities. He'd been faking repentance this entire time.

"You're not sorry at all, are you?"

"Course not. All I did was root through your trash, but you got so mad at me. All you had to do was dodge the knife, but you couldn't even handle that. The two of you messed up my entire life. And for what?!" Yoshinaga started to pull at his hair, glaring at me with a glint of insanity in his eye.

Not only was he unrepentant, he blamed Sayuki and me for what happened. He was holding a grudge. My worst fears were coming true one after the other.

"Stay away from Sayuki."

"Oh no, I'm *so* scared! You can't stop your sister from falling in love with me, y'know!" Yoshinaga stepped up close, smirking in my face.

I could feel the hatred rolling off him in waves.

"Fine. Lucky I already prepared for this."

"What're you gonna do, run to the police? Don't waste your time. I learned in the institution how to sidestep punishments on the fly. I made a ton of friends in there, too."

I didn't know if he was telling the truth or just spitting empty threats. I did know I was playing with fire, though.

"Why are you still stalking her?"

"Why do you think? I'm in love with her. Before, I was too much of a coward to even talk to her, which is why things went so wrong. But I still love her now as much as I did then!" His grin faded, and he lowered his voice. I braced myself. "Y'know, being put away for so long gave me ages to think about stuff. What I'd do when I saw her again. Apologize and ask her to forgive me? Stay away from her and pray for her happiness? Stuff like that. But the more time I spent away from her, the more my feelings grew, and my thoughts started changing."

Yoshinaga paused and looked up at the night sky.

Where's he going with this?

His emotions were all over the place. Right now he was silent and just seemed thoughtful, but my terror grew with each passing second. I wanted to run away so badly. The urge thundered through me, but I thought of Sayuki and knew I couldn't leave.

I'd run away enough over these past ten years. From work, from my family, and from Seika. I was sick of it.

"Even now, I can't stop thinking about Sayuki-san—my sweet Sayuki. I wanna see her crying in front of me, on her knees begging for someone to save her. It's all I ever think about." The excitement in Yoshinaga's voice was barely restrained. His eyes flicked back to me.

He smiled. I'd never seen a smile so unsettling, so evil. This wasn't the kind of guy who should be allowed to walk free. His feelings for Sayuki had broken down into something dark and sinister.

Here I was, alone with this beast. I could still run. I knew I could still run, but I didn't want any more regrets. No more excuses. No more running. I took a step forward. As though he was expecting it, Yoshinaga leaped backwards.

"Whoa, there! What, are you trying to provoke me so you can call the cops?"

That was exactly what I was doing, though not all of it. This man knew how to get away with stuff. I wasn't stupid.

I'd hit the record button on my phone before we even started talking. I was confident I had enough for the police to make a move. If they didn't, I would release this recording online. That could be just as effective as law enforcement these days.

"C'mon, that's not fair. Just when I was trying to turn my life around, too. Though maybe our meeting here is fate, huh? After all, today was the day I was gonna act. Hey, maybe I'll let you participate."

"What are you..."

Yoshinaga raised a hand. I heard footsteps approaching from behind and turned to see the same two men from the minivan closing in on me. The same men I hoped would help me were on *his* side? This was the absolute nightmare scenario.

"These are some of my buddies from the institution. Pretty nasty looking, right? Well, we were planning to send you a video of me getting it on with Sayuki, but I guess having you as a live audience ain't so bad either." Yoshinaga licked his lips.

He was an asshole. A total scumbag. I wanted to punch him in his smirking face, but this was three against one. I couldn't do anything reckless.

Stay calm... Stay calm...

The convenience store was by a road far away from any houses, and I couldn't see anyone else around. Even if I shouted, I couldn't be sure that the store staff would hear me from this distance. Yoshinaga and his cronies knew that, too. He took out a knife. One of the men had a baton and the other a stun gun. They outnumbered me, and they were armed. My legs trembled, and my heart was pounding hard against the walls of my chest.

I was scared, really scared, but I knew that Gams and the rest of my villagers fought against even deadlier foes than this. These weren't monsters or great red goblins—they were just people!

I clenched my fists and took a deep breath.

Come on, guys... Lend me some of that courage!

chapter 06
The Power of Fate and Sayuki's Brother

YOSHINAGA STOOD in front of me, and his two accomplices flanked me from behind. I was surrounded with no hope of escape. The men's faces were different, but they all wore the same repulsive grins. My weight training was always just for show—I wasn't equipped for actual combat. I'd never even punched anyone before! If we fought here, I would lose.

If only I were as strong as Gams, I could easily turn the tables.

I considered what I was dealing with. A knife, a baton, and a stun gun. Of those three dangerous weapons, the stun gun was the biggest problem. If that hit me, I'd be completely powerless. I rolled up my sleeves to show off my large biceps and took up a stance I'd seen in karate videos online. My hands and legs trembled, but I couldn't do anything about that.

"Huh. You're gonna fight, even though you're outnumbered an' unarmed? Yeah, yeah, I can see your muscles, but d'you really think you can win?"

Despite Yoshinaga's words, he seemed unnerved. I was glad that I *looked* strong, at least. Guess my weight training paid off.

I had to use his hesitation to my advantage somehow. This was just like the time my villagers attacked the goblins' camp. I had to use every drop of brainpower I had to come up with a plan.

"Don't try anything clever, or I think you know how this'll end," I said.

"Getting desperate, are we? That's a bad look. But don't worry! My pals here have got pals of their own, if you get what I'm saying. Even if you win, you'd better watch your back."

This was worse than I thought. It might be a bluff, but I couldn't know that for sure.

What I *did* know was this: he hesitated. If he were totally confident in what he was doing, he wouldn't have done that.

"All together now, guys!"

Dammit. Why couldn't they come at me one at a time like in the movies? Why did they have to have common sense?!

All three of them lowered their stances slightly, ready to leap at me. I watched Yoshinaga carefully. The freezing winter wind stung my face and made me shiver, but I held my ground. I knew I wasn't getting out of this. I wasn't Gams. I didn't have the strength to win. Maybe I should just shout and run for the store, hoping for someone to help. It wasn't a courageous way to go, but I was out of courageous options at this point. I lowered my center of gravity and prepared to run.

The two men behind me began to cough.

"A-ah, my throat! A-and...why am I crying?! Wh-what's going on?!" They started gasping, rubbing their eyes and clutching at their throats.

What are they doing?

They flailed and writhed and collapsed to the pavement.

"What the fuck did you do?!" Yoshinaga demanded, waving his knife at me.

He could threaten me all he wanted; I didn't have an answer for him. His accomplices were both twitching on the ground, foaming at the mouth.

Something is...off.

I mean, *obviously*. But it was all I could think about. This was my chance—especially since Yoshinaga looked as confused as me. I pulled my hood low over my face to hide my expression. It was dark enough that he probably couldn't see how freaked out I was. Time to use this sketchy situation against him.

"What do you *think* I did? You really believe I'd roll up and talk to the guy who stabbed me without a backup plan? You should probably get these guys to a hospital, unless you want them to die. If you wanna end up in the same shape, feel free to stick around." I made my voice low and menacing.

I almost kicked the bodies on the ground to scare him even more, but I couldn't bring myself to do it.

"Tell me what you did, dammit! This isn't over!" Yoshinaga raised his arm the same way as before, and two more men got out of the minivan, rushing up to the guys on the floor.

He had more backup, huh?

The van was right in front of the store. If I'd run before, these two would've grabbed me for sure. Keeping his eye on me, Yoshinaga walked around in a wide circle. He tried to haul up one of his twitching teammates, but instead, he collapsed himself.

"Huh?"

It was only now I noticed that his backup was also on the ground. Five men on the ground in front of me, twitching and gasping. The image was so surreal, my brain was having trouble taking it all in.

"...Huh?" I repeated.

Was this an act? Or a prank? Either way, it was freaking me out. I had no qualms about leaving them there, but I didn't want to end up a suspect if they died. I gave them all a light tap on the head, but not one of them responded. I took a few deep breaths to calm myself down, glancing furtively around. No witnesses. I rushed back to the store, feigning panic. Catching sight of the two shop assistants by the counter, I gasped theatrically for breath.

"P-please call the police and an ambulance! Th-there are five guys outside on the ground! Th-they're foaming at the mouth!"

"R-really?!"

"Yeah! They're right there!"

I took one of the assistants out with me to show them. Once they confirmed my story, they immediately got in touch with the emergency services. I was surprised with my acting skills, to be honest...and a little pleased. I wanted to leave things up to the staff and get going, but I was worried they'd check the security cameras and see I was involved. Besides, Sayuki's bus would be here soon. And I wanted to know why Yoshinaga and his men collapsed like that. If I waited, maybe I'd get my answer. I could also pass the recording I took on to the police while I was at it. There were more questions than answers at this point, but at the very least they might arrest Yoshinaga.

"Could you help me carry them?" the store clerk called to me.

"Sure!"

Again pretending I had no idea what happened, I helped the clerk bring the men inside the store, laying them down by the front window. They always said on TV that you weren't supposed to move injured people, but I didn't really care if this damaged their chances of survival. With everyone inside, all we could do was wait for the police and the paramedics to show up. I sipped on the tea that the clerks gave me and waited. People were starting to gather around curiously. We amassed ten or so onlookers, despite how late it was.

"Oniichan? Is that you?"

Sayuki. This crowd must be the people who just got off the bus. The police would probably want to speak to me; maybe I should send Sayuki home first. I could explain to her what happened (or the gist, at least) later.

"It looks like food poisoning or something, but these guys just collapsed. I found them, so I figure the police'll want to talk to me. Why don't you head home, Sayuki? I already asked Dad to come pick you up."

"That's crazy... I'm sorry, Oniichan. You wouldn't have gotten caught up in this if you weren't waiting for me."

"Don't worry about it. I've got the day off tomorrow anyway, and you gotta get up early. D'you mind taking this with you when you go?" As I passed her my backpack, I suddenly remembered something and stuck my hand inside my hoodie.

I'd put the thick magazine I bought earlier in my hoodie pocket, just in case Yoshinaga tried to stab me again. The pages were curled with my sweat. I realized that my hands and knees were still trembling.

"I almost died..." I whispered to myself. The adrenaline was draining from my body, and it was all I could do to keep standing.

The police and ambulance arrived around ten minutes later. Dad showed up at around the same time and took Sayuki home, leaving me with the police to answer how I discovered these men. I told them all about how this guy used to stalk my sister and let them hear the recording. They said they'd launch an investigation straight away. Luckily, the sound cut out when I was threatening them, so I managed to avoid any blame. What they did have was proof that Yoshinaga stalked Sayuki and the details of his planned attack on her. The police took me to the station to ask me some more questions relating to the men's collapse and didn't release me until morning. They even told me off for trying to stand my ground and not calling the police immediately, telling me how much danger I was in, etc.

There was one police officer who praised me, though.

"It's rare to find someone who can keep their cool in a situation like this, and it's easy for others to criticize when they weren't involved. It's tempting to think you'd stay calm, but then when you're actually there, panic takes over and you lose the ability to think clearly."

That officer's words made me feel a little better.

When I left the police station, the morning sun was blazing over the town. I shielded my eyes with my hand and squinted up at the sky.

"Life in the big house really *is* as rough as they say."

That might've been my only chance to say something corny like that, since I wasn't planning on getting arrested any time soon.

"Uh...what?"

"Don't tease him, he's had a rough night."

I turned to find Dad and Sayuki waiting for me.

They heard me! Ugh...

"It's a weekday, right? Why aren't you two at work?"

"Because we were worried! We came to get you! I wouldn't have been able to concentrate at work. And it was sort of because of me that you were here, so...I'm sorry. And, uh...thanks, Oniichan."

I shifted self-consciously at her frank apology. Still, her gratitude made me feel like this had all been worth it.

"Let's go. We shouldn't loiter around the police station for too long."

I got into the back of Dad's car, and Sayuki came to sit next to me. Neither of them said anything, but I could tell they were desperate to ask what happened. I wasn't sure how much to tell them, though. I could pretend it had nothing to do with Sayuki, but if the police came to question her, she'd find out anyway. Hearing about Yoshinaga from me would make the whole thing easier to swallow. I decided to tell them everything.

"It was Yoshinaga?! Didn't that stint in the institution do him any good? What a scumbag!" Sayuki started kicking the passenger seat in front of her.

I couldn't blame her for being angry. He didn't learn his lesson and had gotten even worse over time.

"I understand you're mad, Sayuki, but calm down. And, Yoshio, we're going to have to talk about your reckless behavior," Dad said quietly, words heavy.

He was trying to hold back his anger. The police already gave me an earful, but I was apparently due another.

I should really stop and think before diving in...

"Still, I know you did it all for Sayuki. As your father, I have to admit I'm proud of you."

"Dad..."

Dammit! He's gonna make me cry!

Dad praised me so rarely that I felt my chest fill up with warmth.

"But it's kinda amazing they all collapsed from food poisoning at the same time. Makes me want to thank whoever it is watching over us, even if I don't believe in God," Sayuki said.

Agreed. The "official" reason those five collapsed was still food poisoning. The detective I spoke to mentioned they'd all had oysters for lunch as a pre-celebration party, and those could have done it. I'd never had food poisoning before, so I couldn't judge, but it still made no sense. Not that I had a better explanation. Food poisoning *could* cause foaming at the mouth, I guess, but that didn't explain why they were scratching at their eyes and struggling to breathe. They were acting like people who were poisoned by chemicals, not food. Some kind of gas, maybe? But I knew I only thought of that because of what I'd seen in anime and games. Actual poison was a pretty extreme theory.

"Mmm," I answered, staying noncommittal.

"That's all you've got to say? Oh, wait, I forgot to tell you! Your lizard was in the backpack you gave to me yesterday. You know you've gotta keep it in stable temperatures, right? You can't just take it out on walks in weather like this!"

I stared at her. "Destiny was in the backpack?"

Destiny was with me during the incident? Did that mean...

"No way..."

But I couldn't shake the feeling that I was on to something.

part 6

THE FIRST HINTS
OF SPRING ↵

THE NPCs IN THIS VILLAGE SIM GAME MUST BE REAL! ↵

chapter 01
A Childhood Friend, a Sister, a Lizard, and Me

T HE MOMENT I was home, I raced to my room to check on Destiny, before even glancing at my PC. It was eating some fruit I assumed Dad or Sayuki gave it, but its dinner wasn't the issue. It was with me last night. Maybe it crawled into my backpack looking for a place to stay warm?

"Destiny, did you do...whatever that was last night?" I looked it in its huge, round eyes.

It stared back for a brief second before returning its attention to the fruit.

"Right...what am I thinking? Lizards can't do that kinda stuff. Hey, Destiny, I'm sorry for not paying you enough attention, but d'you mind not hiding in places like that? Sayuki said I should keep you out of the cold."

Leaving Destiny to its fruit, I sat in front of my PC. My villagers were working hard, and everything seemed peaceful. Murus didn't let her emotions show on her face, but sometimes I caught her staring up at the sky or wistfully into the forest. Healing would take time.

I checked through the backlog to see if anything had happened while I was gone, but I didn't find anything interesting. The whole stalking incident messed me up so much, I worried that I might've forgotten something important, so I cast my mind back to what happened in my village the day before.

My villagers went to Murus's village and met Dordold, the merchant. They collected a ton of necessities to help them through the winter. Rodice mentioned they had plenty to last the season now, even if they did end up taking more people in.

I'd performed so many miracles lately that my villagers' gratitude towards me had increased, meaning I had a lot of FP saved up. I used a fair bit controlling that tiny statue, but it didn't cost nearly as much as the 1,000 FP for summoning the full-sized golem. I didn't know if that was because it was smaller or because it cost less the second time. Either way, it still wasn't cheap. I'd need to spend sparingly.

"If only I were rich enough to use miracles whenever I wanted. Sorry, guys. Your God's broke."

Having less money did make it seem more valuable, in a way. My game was important, but I did want to put some of my wages towards my family, too. That's what stopped me from spamming miracles until my wallet ran dry. I didn't want to get in the habit of constantly doing microtransactions, either. I needed just enough FP to save my villagers from any trouble they encountered.

I sighed and looked at the screen. Carol was helping Lyra and Chem with some chores, while Rodice went through the items they'd collected from Murus's village and bought from Dordold.

Murus and Gams were out patrolling the area. As always, my villagers were working hard for their survival. I couldn't help but think that adding more FP to my virtual wallet could help them live more comfortably.

"Dordold said he'd be back in a few weeks, and he might have someone with him who wants to join the village. I wonder what they'll be like."

Any other game and I would've welcomed a scantily clad witch or a hot female knight, but my village really needed more fighters and manpower. This game felt less like a pastime and more like a responsibility, and I couldn't afford to be selfish when it came to my village's survival. What I really needed was a powerful fighter or a specialized craftsman. My villagers mentioned as much when Dordold asked them what sort of people they were looking for.

"Those are our preferences," Rodice said. "But we are willing to accept anybody who has lost their home and will do their share. If you would prioritize anybody who came from our village, we would be incredibly grateful. Oh, and Murus's village, as well."

That meant we might get some useless people added to our ranks, although I didn't mean that to be as harsh as it sounded. And I agreed with Rodice's proposal. The best case scenario would be if my villagers already knew the newcomers.

My top pick would be a woman who was skilled, beautiful, and powerful, even if it meant adding another person to Chem and Carol's feud. Poor Gams. Popularity was a curse.

"Yoshio!" Mom called from downstairs.

Both Dad and Sayuki stayed home from work today out of concern for me, so for once, everyone was here on a weekday, but I checked the time and it was still too early for lunch.

"Maybe I got a package."

I went downstairs to find Okiku-baachan and Seika drinking tea under the kotatsu in the living room. Okiku-baachan wore a kimono, and Seika was dressed more casually in black-framed glasses and a white turtleneck. It suited her. She had a great body, and that sweater emphasized her chest. I mean, so did all the well-fitting clothes she wore. I realized I was staring and looked quickly away. I hadn't been expecting her to show up on a weekday.

"You're not working today?"

"Oh, Yoshio-kun. Sayuki-chan said you were in some trouble, so I came to check up on you. I took the day off."

If she weren't working for such a big, successful company, I doubted that was a good enough reason for her to skip.

"Right. Well, I'm sure she told you everything, but you don't need to worry. I'm fine." I sat down opposite Seika and gave Okiku-baachan a polite nod.

She smiled at me, the wrinkles on her face crumpling, and offered me a piece of candy. She did this every time we met, ever since I was a kid. Apparently, it was customary in Kansai, where she grew up. I thanked her and put it in my mouth. It was my favorite kind... Was that a coincidence, or did she remember?

"Okiku-san, I'm having trouble with my sewing! Could you help me, please?"

"Of course, dearie! I'm on my way!" Okiku-baachan went to join Mom in the other room, leaving Seika, Sayuki, and me under the kotatsu.

"Hey, where's Dad?" I asked.

"He got called back to work. It was urgent, apparently," Sayuki said.

"Sounds annoying."

I trailed off awkwardly. I had no idea how to speak to Seika anymore. At least she and Sayuki still saw each other regularly and had a rapport. Hopefully that'd make things easier on me.

They weren't getting the message, though. They were just sipping their tea in silence.

Somebody say something!

Maybe *I* should say something. I racked my brain for a topic of conversation.

"So, uh...Seika. Did Sayuki tell you everything about last night?"

"More or less. That guy was her old stalker, right? And he was going to kidnap her or something, but then you showed up, Yoshio-kun, and—"

"You can just call me Yoshi if it's easier."

"Kun" was a little much, since we were both over thirty, but I wasn't going to push it.

"Really? Oh, thanks." She smiled bashfully, and I found myself staring at her again.

Seika was way too cute for a woman her age. Maybe she looked younger than she was, or maybe it was just that her mannerisms made me nostalgic.

"Sorry to ruin the mood, but the whole stalker thing is over now, right?" Sayuki leaned forward over the kotatsu.

She looked a little annoyed, steering us away from nicknames and back to the very real danger she was in. I knew it had weighed on her mind for a long time.

"You should be fine now. The guy's in the hospital, but the police said he's going straight to jail the moment he's out. Apparently, he had messages about the plan on his phone. Added to the recording I took, that's plenty of evidence."

He'd stabbed me when he was thirteen and therefore never stood trial or earned a criminal record. But since he and his gang all came out of the institution, the police assured me they would be punished. Exactly how remained to be seen. Whatever happened, Yoshinaga wouldn't be causing any more harm for a long while.

"I think we can rely on the police to do their job this time."

One of the younger detectives at the station was extra nice to me, and we ended up chatting for a while. He told me he had a relative who'd been stalked and could sympathize. He even promised to contact me about any developments in the case.

"That's a huge relief." Sayuki flopped down on top of the kotatsu. She was the kind of person who always did her best to smile, but I could tell a weight had been lifted off her shoulders.

"Listen, if anything like this happens again, you just let me know, 'kay?"

"I will. Thanks, Oniichan."

"Aww, it's just like old times!" Seika giggled and smiled warmly.

The three of us used to play together all the time, and Seika saw Sayuki as her sister, too. She looked genuinely overjoyed that the two of us were on good terms again.

"Old times, huh?" Sayuki glanced at me awkwardly.

"I'd like to think so," I said.

"Y-yeah. Me too." Sayuki nodded twice, as though trying to convince herself.

She was self-conscious, but I was relieved that she agreed. She also seemed happy that Sayuki and I had patched things up.

I couldn't erase those lost years when my sister and I despised each other, but I was done wallowing in regrets. I only cared about moving forward, no matter how slow my progress was.

"What about us, Yoshi? Wanna go back to how we were?"

I felt a small tug on my sleeve and turned to find Seika blinking up at me. How the heck was I supposed to say no to a face like that?!

"Of course. I mean, I should be the one asking you. I'm sorry for what I said. I'd like to pick up where we left off." I put my hands on the kotatsu and lowered my head.

Seika had found a great job with a decent company almost straight away while I struggled with rejection after rejection. I was jealous and took it out on her. I said something *awful* to her.

If I could turn back time, I'd go back just to punch myself in the face.

Guess that's another regret, huh?

"Don't worry! I forgive you!"

I looked up, taken aback by the cheerful note in her reply. She grinned at me, a cheeky glint in her eye.

"You're real high-maintenance, you know that?"

"I'm sorry. I really thought I made you hate me."

"Of course I didn't *hate* you. But I got transferred and had to move off, and even when I came back, I was always away on business. And, to be honest, I... Wait, never mind."

She had me curious, but this was already awkward enough with Sayuki right here. She clearly wasn't enjoying being ignored.

I was scared that Seika had long since given up on me, but here she was now, reaching out to make amends. It wasn't just my family I took for granted these past ten years, while I avoided everything to protect my fragile pride. I certainly had more failures waiting for me in the future, but I wouldn't let that scare me.

"Maybe we should go somewhere, and—" Suddenly, Seika let out a yelp and shuffled back towards the window. The color had drained from her face. I looked over to see what had frightened her so badly.

"You got out *again*?" I scooped Destiny up in my hands and set it gently on top of the kotatsu.

Seika shook her head frantically, tears forming in her eyes.

Right, she doesn't like reptiles.

I picked Destiny up again and pointed the lizard in her direction with a grin.

"S-stop that, Yoshi! We're not kids anymore! You know I hate snakes and lizards and stuff!"

Oops. She was super pissed.

THE NPCs IN THIS VILLAGE SIM GAME MUST BE REAL! ↵

chapter 02 The Villagers' Advice and Their Unsure God—Part 1

AFTER SEVERAL YEARS of not being in contact, I was finally speaking to Seika normally again. I couldn't be happier, but I still struggled to come up with topics of conversation. We promised to go back to how we were, but that couldn't happen overnight, especially after what I said to her all those years ago.

When she found that job, I congratulated her, of course, but inside I was panicked and annoyed.

"I'm gonna focus on finding a job, so please don't contact me until then."

After I said that, I stopped messaging her completely. The truth was...I was jealous, and I didn't want her to know. I only applied to jobs that were on her level or better...and I didn't get any of them. As I sank into the endless pit of unemployment, I felt worse about myself, and that put even more distance between us. My motivation waned, my heart hardened, and the years passed. So much time spent avoiding responsibility made me into who I was now. After all that, what was I supposed to say to Seika?

How was I supposed to act with her? I had enough trouble talking to my family. All my bad decisions had caught up to me.

At least I was used to voice chat. I spent a lot of time during the years talking with allies in online games.

"I guess it's fine as long as I don't have to look anyone in the eye. But even then..."

I'd phoned Seika a few times back then, but I was nervous and never knew what to say. I couldn't even remember what we talked about. And trying to instant message or email just made me feel worse for my lack of real-life communication skills. Was there any clearer sign that you were a shut-in than excelling at text messages?

"I guess I've still got a long way to go."

I thought I'd made huge progress by talking with Sayuki and my coworkers, but when it came to Seika, my nerves took over. Muscle memory from our years as best friends was the only reason I could speak to her at all.

"Talking is hard."

There had to be a way to practice. As always, I was sitting in my chair, gazing at the computer screen and my hardworking villagers.

"Maybe these guys can help me out."

They were great at forming strong bonds with each other and outsiders. Even Gams, who struggled with words, didn't do too badly. I could use him as a model.

As though reading my mind, Carol rushed up to him to start a conversation.

"What are you doing today, Gams?"

"I'll be heading out with Murus soon."

"Murus, huh?" Carol's radiant smile faded into an expression that looked a lot like the look on Chem's face whenever Gams gave Carol—in her opinion—too much attention.

"Don't be gone too long, okay? And don't get hurt!" Carol said.

"Sure." Gams smiled and patted her head gently.

Carol smiled back. She seemed happy, but I knew I shouldn't just copy Gams's behavior. Only good-looking guys could get away with patting girls on the head. You saw it all the time in anime and stuff, but trying it in real life would be creepy and just piss the girl off.

Now that I thought about it, Gams rarely initiated conversation, and his replies were always curt. "Sure" or "Yeah." He could go whole days without forming a single sentence. Maybe Rodice would be a better role model for me, since his job involved talking to people. He had a wife and a kid, too, so he had at least *some* degree of responsibility. I scanned the area for the merchant.

"Where are you, Rodice? Not outside, so... Oh! There he is!"

He sat working at the wooden dining table while Lyra washed the dishes nearby. Chem was polishing my wooden statue. Suddenly, she looked toward the cave entrance and frowned. Packing up her cleaning tools, she hurried outside.

Wonder what got to her? Argh, never mind.

"Did you finish sorting those documents, dear?" Lyra put down the last dish and walked over to her husband.

He's writing that list, huh?

Rodice had told Dordold that he would put together a list of products my villagers were willing to sell and ones they were looking to buy. He sent the merchant off with a short list, then set about making a more comprehensive document once he'd had time to check the cave's storage.

"They're basically done. I'm so glad we met Dordold. I kept thinking I'd go out to the nearest town to sell some of our surplus, but I never got the chance. Running into a merchant was fortunate indeed."

"Perhaps the Lord led us to him."

"I like to think so."

Rodice and Lyra approached the altar to give me a prayer of thanks. Though not as devout as Chem, their faith was strong, and they never missed their daily prayers. They were right about me leading them to Dordold, but most days they thanked me for stuff I had nothing to do with. I felt a little guilty about it.

"I'm not as powerful as you guys think I am."

In fact, as deities went, I was pathetic. But pathetic or not, I'd do everything I could for my villagers. It wasn't their fault they were stuck with me as their God.

"Don't push yourself too hard," Lyra said. "There's no point working until you collapse."

"I know that. It's just, seeing how much Gams does makes me want to do better." Rodice put his pen on the table and sighed. "I'm the oldest person here, but I'm still practically useless."

I knew just how he felt. Gams fought off monsters and did a ton of physical labor every day, and he never complained one bit.

Even *I* wanted to work harder when I watched him, and I was the laziest guy on the planet. I wasn't surprised that Rodice, who lived in the same world as him, was constantly comparing himself to Gams. Rodice wasn't as useless as he claimed, though. He put in a lot of work himself, doing what he could with his frailer body, not afraid to break a sweat. Just like Gams, he never complained, pushing himself to his absolute physical limits and sleeping like the dead afterward. Every day, again and again.

The way I saw it, Rodice was just as much of a man as Gams.

"And I don't want Gams stealing our little Carol away from us, either!"

Oh. So that's what it was. That made sense. Fathers were often overprotective.

"Oh, darling." Lyra walked up to her fretting husband and laid a gentle hand on his shoulder. "It's too late to worry about that."

Ouch!

Rodice's shoulders drooped several inches. I mean, Lyra was right, but she didn't have to say it!

"Come now, it's not so bad. Children are fated to leave their parents' side sooner or later."

"Maybe...but she's only seven!"

"You have me, don't you?"

"Yes. I do."

Were all couples like this? Lyra always seemed like a self-reliant, powerful woman, but when she was alone with Rodice she could really switch on the charm. The two of them seemed to be radiating a sickly pink aura as they stared into each other's eyes. I decided it was time to look away from the cave. Lyra had a tendency to act more like Rodice's mother than his wife, but they sure could get flirty with each other when they were alone. It made me cringe, but that didn't mean I wasn't a little jealous.

"Looks like I'm done learning from Rodice, anyway."

This wasn't going as smoothly as I hoped. I didn't have anyone to ask about how to talk to women in real life, either. Sayuki was out—if I asked her about Seika, she'd probably laugh at me. I had an online friend who always boasted about being great with women, but for someone with such a fulfilling love life, he sure was on the computer a lot. We were all too polite to point it out.

"Oh, I should probably send 'em today's prophecy."

I was so wrapped up in my social problems I nearly forgot. Even if I had nothing important to say, I sent them a message every single day.

"Might just send them something vague again, and... Wait a sec."

Maybe I could ask my villagers for advice! I'd need to be careful to remain divine, of course, but it might work. I came up with a brief message and typed it in. After editing it for godliness, I hit the enter button.

"Everyone! The daily prophecy's here!" Chem called.

I waited till everyone was at the cave and taking a break to send it, so none of them would be too busy to listen.

"Ready? Here goes. 'Today, I have something to ask of my loyal followers. A young follower is having trouble with his love life. Unfortunately, I am not familiar with love and romance between humans, and so I would ask you for your advice.' Oh..." Chem paused in confusion, reading the prophecy over a few times.

The other villagers looked just as perplexed.

"Chem, is the Lord asking us for romantic advice?" Lyra asked with a frown.

"I believe so. I read it a few times, but there's no doubt about it. He appears to be asking on behalf of one of His followers."

I might've gotten ahead of myself a bit—it really *was* a weird question for a god to ask. I should've put more thought into the words, but it was too late now. All I could do was come up with some excuse to cover my tracks tomorrow.

"Does that mean God listens to our romantic troubles?" Carol asked. "Can I ask Him about my love life?"

"Quiet, Carol. You mustn't trouble the Lord with trivial things. I shall ask Him first, to make sure it's okay."

"No fair! You're gonna steal my man!"

"Where on earth did you learn language like *that*?"

Luckily, Chem and Carol's bickering seemed to have distracted them from their suspicions. I wasn't looking forward to answering any prayers about poor Gams, though. Whoever I sided with, someone would be hurt.

"Now, now, you two! Don't forget that the Lord has asked us a question! We rely on Him so much, and now we finally have an opportunity to pay Him back! We must think seriously about our answer!" Lyra said.

"I'm afraid I won't be able to contribute much," Murus said. "I'm not familiar with human romance..."

With Lyra and Murus on board, at least I knew they were taking me seriously. Well, the women were, at least. Gams and Rodice had stepped away from the group to watch from afar. I'd probably do the same in their position. This kind of thing was best left to the girls...even if it was a little weird to see two grown men acting like the guys at school, intimidated by girls talking about romance and crushes and stuff. I guess love talk was generally more popular with girls in any world.

The only question now was whether my villagers would come up with anything good.

chapter 03 The Villagers' Advice and Their Unsure God—Part 2

"**C**OULD YOU READ US the rest of the prophecy, Chem?"

I didn't expect Lyra to be the most excited of all of them, but I was grateful. She was married and had the most romantic experience. If anyone could give me good advice, it would be her.

"Of course. Let's see...the man has a childhood friend. Apparently, they're closer than ordinary friends but not quite lovers. They've been together almost their whole lives and know each other better than anyone! That sounds so wonderful!" As Chem spoke, her tone became more adamant.

Maybe she was trying to send Carol a message.

"If they're always together, they're probably sick of each other!" Carol tilted her head in mock thoughtfulness.

I knew she was trying to provoke Chem, but it was just adorable. She gave as good as she got, and to be honest, it was hard to remember she was just a seven-year-old child.

"Save your bickering for later, you two. There's more, isn't there, Chem?" Lyra asked firmly, pulling the two of them apart.

Murus watched them with an awkward smile, holding her silence.

"Oh! Please excuse me. Well, they were apart for a few years but recently reestablished contact. However, the man isn't sure how to speak to her or how to go back to the relationship they had all those years ago."

At that, the women fell silent and started to think. They were taking this so seriously that my gratitude was turning into guilt. Was this an abuse of power?

"I know! I know!" Carol thrust her hand up in the air, a huge grin on her face.

"Perhaps you should take some more time to think. Romance is a very complicated subject," Chem warned her.

"Yeah, I know that! I was super popular with the boys back in the village! I got way more experience than you!" Carol insisted, her little cheeks puffed out in anger.

Given how cheerful and cute she was, I could believe that she was popular with her peers. Chem staggered backward and clutched at her chest at Carol's jab. She probably didn't associate with many boys. Her fierce-looking brother likely drove them away.

"Very well. If you're so confident, let us hear your opinion."

"They should go on a date!" Carol declared.

Easier said than done, Carol!

"I'm not sure. It seems a little too soon for that, considering he can't even talk to her properly."

"Huh? But they used to talk all the time! So I think they should go on a date! Then, if there's no spark, he can give up on her!"

She was weirdly insistent for someone barely out of diapers. Chem shot Lyra a questioning glance, which Lyra avoided.

"Okay, no more romance stories for you before bedtime. Picture books only from now on!"

Seemed like it was Lyra's fault. I wondered what sort of stuff she was reading to her daughter.

"I have to admit your suggestion makes sense, Carol. Having a fun time together will clear things up quicker than several awkward encounters."

"I think so, too. Rodice and I wouldn't be where we are today if he never asked me on that first date!"

"Now, Lyra, I don't think there's any need to talk about that!" Rodice cut in quickly, his face red.

"Do you have any opinions, Murus?" Chem asked the elf, who was listening with a serious expression.

"Well...we elves take a long time to cultivate our romances. It's rare for us to be so upfront about everything. I'm sorry, but I don't think I'm the right person to ask."

Sounded like elves' love lives were as leisurely as their life spans.

So Carol thinks I should ask Seika on a date...

Seika and I used to go out together a lot before we stopped hanging out. We'd see movies, go to the beach or the park, but we were adults now. If I took her on a date, it would need to be fancy, like a restaurant with a view of the sea. Not a chain, either; a fancy independent place. Maybe French?

This wasn't working. I'd never been anywhere like that, and I couldn't even imagine what it would be like. I was just thinking of scenes from dramas and anime. What kinds of dates were thirty-year-olds supposed to go on? And that was assuming Seika even *wanted* to go on a date with me.

"As long as he was happy when we were together, that's all I'd need!"

"Gams is happy when he's with me! So that means we should go on a date, right?!"

"Of course not!"

The dreamy look on Chem's face disappeared instantly at Carol's proposal, and her tone grew icy. I usually thought she was too harsh towards the little girl, but at this point, Carol was actively antagonizing Chem. I almost suspected that she must be hiding behind her youth to avoid blame. Hopefully that was just my imagination.

"Men can be adorable when they're trying their best to look all nice for you. They try hard to be manly, and it hardly ever works! Right, dear?"

"Please...no more..." Rodice buried his burning face in his hands.

Murus continued to listen, nodding thoughtfully at each new point. I almost expected her to pull out a notepad and start taking notes. The love affairs of humans seemed to fascinate her.

Gams never said a word, and I never expected him to. In the end, the girls agreed that this "follower" of mine should invite the girl on a date and see how things went. I sighed. I knew their advice was earnest, but there was no way I could follow it. It was just too soon to think about a date. I didn't want to put their advice to waste either, though, so I pulled out my phone.

"'Hey, how're you doing?' No, I can't write that... 'Are you free right now?' No, that's too basic..."

The seconds ticked by, and I was still no closer to sending Seika a message.

"If you're free right now, wanna do something?"

That was what I finally came up with—the same sort of text I sent when we were kids. Not *exactly* a date invitation, but I did appreciate my villagers taking my problem so seriously. I slid out of my chair and knelt on the floor before bowing toward my computer.

Sorry, guys! I can't take your advice!

I'd been estranged from Seika for years. I couldn't invite her on a date out of the blue, especially considering how long it took me to come up with the simplest message.

"Well, I did my best," I sighed. Suddenly I felt a strange sensation.

Looking up, I found Destiny sitting on the edge of my desk and leaning forward to pat my head.

"Are you...proud of me?" I felt a warm glow in my chest. "Thanks. H-hey, what are you doing?"

I felt one claw on my head, then two, then its entire body weight. It proceeded to curl up in my hair. Maybe it wasn't proud of me after all. It *was* only a lizard. I would've been happy to let it stay there, but I was getting hungry, so I picked it up gently and put it on my desk. When I stood to head down to the kitchen, my phone beeped. I snatched it up to see a message from Seika.

"That was quick," I said casually, but my hands were already damp with sweat.

I knew I had to read it, if only to politely reply if she rejected me. Taking a deep breath, I opened the message.

"Thanks for the invitation, but you know it's the middle of the day on a weekday, right? I'm at work! Let's meet up another time, okay?"

Wait...it's a weekday?

I checked the calendar; it was indeed a weekday. In my defense, it was years since I needed to know the day of the week.

"Sorry to disturb you when you're busy. I'll message you again another time."

I sent my response. Somehow, I felt both disappointed and relieved at the same time. From her response, she didn't seem averse to the idea of going somewhere with me. If I invited her out again when she wasn't busy, that meant she'd say yes, right?

At the end of all of that, nothing really came of my efforts. I'd just have to try again another time.

The next day, my villagers were *still* talking about yesterday's prophecy.

"What do you think happened to that man who asked God for help?" Carol asked Lyra as she helped her mother with the washing.

"Who knows? I'm sure we weren't the only ones the Lord came to for advice."

"Do you think he asked that girl on a date?"

Sorry, kiddo, but it didn't work out...

"I can't help being curious myself," Chem cut in, a basket full of wet washing in her arms.

"Yeah! I hope they get back together!"

"Me too."

It warmed my heart to see them agreeing for once. As long as Gams wasn't around, they were both perfectly capable of being civil.

I didn't expect everyone to be this interested in the outcome. Maybe I should let them know what happened in today's prophecy.

"I won't focus too much on the rejection—just thank them for their advice. It'd be rude not to tell them how things turned out."

I did just that, not saying outright that the "young man" was rejected. They were delighted that they had been of use to their God.

"You guys do more for me than you realize. Thank you."

After that second prophecy, romance became even more of a hot topic within the cave, and the girls were constantly sharing their ideas. They smiled as they chatted, not even getting angry when the others disagreed with them. Gams and Rodice would watch them with awkward smiles, but they seemed to be enjoying it in their own way.

"They're a lot more into this than I thought they'd be. I don't see what's so fascinating about all this love stuff myself..."

Well, as long as they were happy, it didn't really matter. I still didn't get it, though. They were behaving the exact same way Mom and Sayuki did when they watched those TV dramas together. My villagers rarely talked about anything else anymore, even when they were working.

"It's a shame the Lord didn't give us the exact outcome of the situation. I just hope it all went well," said Chem.

"Me too," Lyra agreed. "It would be a nice change from all the doom and gloom we hear about out here."

Wait, now I get it! This is their only source of entertainment!

They worked so hard to keep their village running every single day that they never had time to have fun. I hadn't considered that. I mean, what could they even do as a leisure activity? The world outside the fence was so dangerous, and they were stuck in that cave all day, every day. That was exactly why Gams insisted on Rodice and his family accompanying them to Murus's village.

"I can't believe I didn't see it. I'm so dense!"

I could regret it later. For the time being, I would just learn as much as I could about human relationships from the villagers. Maybe I should tell them exactly what happened with Seika so that they'd have more to talk about. I didn't like exposing my vulnerabilities, but if it kept them entertained, it was worth it. I decided this wouldn't be the last time I'd ask them for advice.

chapter 04 The Villagers' Advice and Their Unsure God—Part 3

"**T**HE PROPHECY IS HERE! Everybody gather 'round!" Chem called out excitedly.

The other women rushed up to her, dropping their important tasks without a thought.

"The Lord let us know what happened to that young man with romance troubles."

Lyra and the others cheered. Rodice and Gams glanced behind them briefly before they went back to reinforcing the log fence. It didn't escape my notice that they paused their work, though. Like they were listening intently.

"Here goes! 'The young man has asked for my advice once more, so I would like to hand it over to my dear followers of the cave. Here is what he asked of me...'"

I tried to write the first part in my godlike voice but then changed to quoting my "follower" directly so I didn't have to worry so much about my language.

"'My childhood friend said she'd hang out with me. But I don't know where we should go! I live in the city so there are loads of places and restaurants we could go to, but I don't know which one I should pick to make her happy. I don't even know what to wear! I'm sorry, Lord…I know it's rude to ask your advice on something so silly…but please help me!'" Having read out the prophecy, Chem sighed.

She looked so thoughtful that I worried I'd messed up somehow.

"The rest is written in the Lord's voice. 'My job is to govern the fates of mankind. Romantic relationships are a part of that fate, thus I cannot turn my back on this young man. It would please me greatly to hear your opinions.' That's where it stops." Chem looked up, her eyes sparkling as she clutched her holy book to her chest with another sigh.

"Oh, to be young and in love!" Lyra grinned.

"We gotta help him, everyone!" Carol shouted importantly.

Murus nodded thoughtfully several times.

Looks like I'm in for some more advice!

"That means she said yes to the date, doesn't it? I'm so glad to hear it! Now he just needs to decide where the date should be!"

"What's a city?" Carol asked, tugging on Lyra's sleeve.

"It's like a town but with a lot more people!"

"How many people? One hundred? One thousand?" Carol stretched out her arms to demonstrate.

"Many, many more than that!" Lyra laughed.

For a girl who'd never left her village, that must be impossible to imagine.

"Rodice and I used to go shopping in the city all the time. They have everything you could ever want!"

I couldn't help wondering what the city in the game world was like. If it was anything like the fantasy anime I'd seen, it was probably a huge walled metropolis. In a world with monsters, you needed high walls to protect your dwellings. Maybe it was surrounded by a moat full of water, like the kind around Japanese castles.

That was exactly what my dream village would look like in this game. Big stone walls with a deep moat around them, a gate at each compass point and drawbridges that the villagers could pull up. A perfect, defensible structure. It'd probably take years to get to that point from here, though.

"Let's backtrack a little. Say you were going on a date in the city. Where would you like to go?" Lyra asked.

"I wanna go buy clothes, and Gams can pick them out for me!"

"You want to dress to his tastes?" Rodice asked. "I don't remember raising such a crafty daughter..."

"Yeah, but then I'll pick what he wears, and then we can wear them together!"

Did she forget this was supposed to be advice for someone else? Carol buried her face in her hands and started to squirm as she imagined how the rest of their date would go. I was waiting for Chem to say something, but she was too deep in thought. She stared into space and then suddenly broke into a grin.

"Choosing clothes and going on a date with Gams...that's not bad!"

All she'd done was steal Carol's idea and insert herself in as Gams's date.

"What do you think, Murus, since those two aren't being helpful?" Lyra turned to the elf.

"Well, I can't be entirely sure, but perhaps he should choose somewhere the two of them can talk?"

"I don't think that would work. Talking is what he has a problem with in the first place." Lyra smiled gently at Murus. Lyra was the most reliable villager for this situation. "Although, you might be right. Perhaps he could take some time to talk to her and find out what she likes to do, and then things will be easier. Don't you think so, dear?"

"Ow!" Rodice shook out his hand—he'd managed to miss the nail and hit his finger instead.

He was *listening!*

"This isn't going anywhere. Why don't we break the problem down?" Chem suggested. "First, he needs somewhere to take her. I'd like to suggest the theater."

"That's perfect! That was where Rodice and I had our first date! We went to see a romantic play together, and the dimly-lit atmosphere was so lovely!"

Rodice started coughing loudly, clearly hoping it would stop her.

"I wanna see a play, too!"

"Not a bad idea."

It even had Gams's approval!

The theater, huh? In this world, a movie theater would probably be more appropriate. Should we go see a romance film? I didn't really like them, but I imagined Seika might. I could try and slip the question into a conversation later.

"Next, we should think about his fashion choices. Something neat and tidy should do the trick! He should put in a little more effort than usual for a date," Chem said, glancing over at Gams.

She was obviously imagining him in something a bit "neater".

"I wanna see Gams all dressed up!"

"Me too!" Chem added, the two of them in rare agreement.

Gams shivered and glanced up, like he could feel stares on his back.

Turn around Gams. They're right there!

"I prefer something a little rougher around the edges. He should try to be himself," Lyra said. Her opinion was definitely a little more mature than the others'.

"I agree with Lyra," Murus said. "He should try to act natural."

Their ideas were split right down the middle. The problem was that I had no idea which Seika would prefer. She was closer to Lyra in age, so maybe I should go with casual.

The female villagers' discussion lasted for about an hour. I made note of anything that seemed useful and then took a break from the computer. I was exhausted! Way more exhausted than I thought I'd be just listening to people talk.

"At least I got some good advice."

Maybe I'd talk to Seika tonight. I was armed with more knowledge than last time, so this should be easier. And wanting to report back to my villagers was a big motivator.

This would be fine. I used to invite her out like it was nothing. I just had to channel the me from ten years ago.

After dinner, I went back to my room and had a staring contest with my phone.

"She's gotta be back from work by now, right?"

I moved to the window and glanced toward Seika's house. The lights were on in her room. She had to be home. There was no excuse not to call her.

I could just leave it and not say anything about it in the prophecy tomorrow. But then I imagined the disappointed looks on their faces when they realized they weren't getting an update.

"I gotta have something to tell them..." I grabbed my phone and opened my contacts list.

Seika answered after three rings.

"Yoshi? It's been ages since you last called me!"

"Yeah... Hey, listen, about that message I sent at lunch..."

"Everyone! The prophecy is here!"

The female villagers all dropped whatever they were doing and gathered around Chem before she could even finish her sentence.

"Here goes. 'The young man said to thank you for your advice. Because of your words, he has advanced his relationship. I am very grateful for your help and shall not require advice on this matter any longer.'"

Chem finished reading and smiled along with the others. Even Gams and Rodice looked pleased as they watched from afar.

I was glad that the prophecies entertained them, but I couldn't keep things going and forget the real point of the game. The prophecy was supposed to be for relaying essential information, not for helping me fix my life. This would be the last time I asked them for advice, at least for now.

"Back to normal tomorrow, guys."

Maybe one day the dangers in their world would settle, and I could send a prophecy like that every day. That would be nice.

But if I wanted to get there, I had to focus on the village's development. I still had plenty of time before this month's Day of Corruption, but I wanted to be as prepared as possible. There was also no telling when Dordold might return with some new villagers. We had plenty to work on besides my personal life.

"I'm gonna go to work so I have money for you guys...and money for my date."

I pulled on my coveralls and waved goodbye to my villagers before leaving my room. I was determined to work hard, both for my villagers and for myself.

part 7

THE SHADOW THREATENING

MY PEACEFUL LIFE ↵

THE NPCs IN THIS VILLAGE SIM GAME MUST BE REAL! ↵

chapter 01
A Real Village and My Sense of Satisfaction

TWO WEEKS HAD PASSED since Murus joined my village, and December was slowly coming to a close. Only a week remained of the year. Up until now I'd been working an average of three times a week, but the end of the year was especially busy, with companies hiring us to do deep cleans. We all had December 30th and 31st off, but all the rest of the time my coworkers were working hard, and I had more shifts, too. I was scheduled to work five days out of this final week of the year. I was making money, and I didn't want to waste it. I was going to save whatever I could.

I'd been working this job for a while now, but it was only recently I realized how well it suited me. Watching a floor become cleaner and cleaner as you worked on it was extremely satisfying. It wasn't all sunshine and rainbows, though. Working outside or in an office when the heating was off sucked, but my villagers taught me that work wasn't always easy. They never quit and didn't complain. It was winter in the game, too, and all they had to keep them warm was a small fire. By their standards, I was lucky.

Speaking of the village, our long-awaited newcomers came to join us recently.

"It's good to see you all again! I hope you've been well."

Dordold arrived at the cave with his guards and a large cart pulled by two horses. He stopped the cart just outside the fence.

"Welcome, Dordold." Gams opened the gate in the corner of the fence for him.

"The fenced-in area has gotten larger since I was last here! You could do a bit of building here or sow a patch of farmland. I am so looking forward to seeing what you do with it!"

I was impressed he remembered how big the plot was, considering he'd only been there once before. My villagers had toiled to move the fence outward and make space for any new arrivals. It now enclosed a space twice as big as before. They even built a stable for their two horses, moving them out of the cave and finally freeing my villagers from the constant smell of manure. The work was only recently finished; Dordold had showed up at just the right time.

"I brought the items you asked for. Check them over when you have time, yeah? Oh, and I brought two new members for your village! If you'll have them." Dordold waved a hand at the cart, and two figures stepped out.

They looked nearly identical, just a bit taller than Carol, coming up to around Gams's waist. Their faces were big, and their limbs stocky. The bags on their backs were bigger than they were and filled with wooden stalks. Their short-sleeved tops and short pants were made of leather and sewn with pockets. The legs and arms poking out were covered in brown fur. So were their faces. Their eyes were large and round, and the area around their eyes, cheeks, and mouth was white. Their noses were wide and snout-like.

"They look like red pandas! Though they're standing on two feet..."

They even had little tufty tails on their butts. I'd be lying if I said they were anything but extremely adorable. I knew their giant, black-and-white cousins were the more popular and well known kind of panda, but I preferred the red variety, so their appearance was a very welcome surprise.

"This is Kan and Lan. They are bearcats, and a married couple."

"I'm Kan."

"I'm Lan."

The two creatures bowed their heads. They were very human-like, so that's how I'd treat them. Discrimination against beastfolk was a common trope in fantasy settings. I wondered whether it would be the same in this world.

"Bearcats!" Chem exclaimed, running up to them and taking their ha—paws. "You're very welcome here."

"Fluffy!" Carol was scrambling around them, clearly dying to touch their fur.

I knew just how she felt. I bet their paws were all soft and squishy, too...

"Damn, I wish I were there right now! I just wanna bury my face in their fur and rub against it. If only they were my pets..."

I preferred smaller animals to big ones, and I always wanted a cat, but Dad was allergic.

I just couldn't keep my eyes off Kan and Lan!

I felt a heavy weight of disapproval and turned to find Destiny glaring at me as it sat on the rim of its tank. Uh oh! Did it hear me?

"Uh, you got it wrong, Destiny! I wasn't, uh... Hey, do you want some fruit?"

I offered it the plate of fruit I brought up here for myself, but it dismissed me with a wave of its tail. It went back into the tank, rolled itself into a ball, and ignored me.

Come on. With that attitude, it *had* to understand what I was saying.

I guess that doesn't matter if it won't listen, though.

Unable to do anything else, I left the fruit inside the tank and decided to play with Destiny when it was in a better mood. I sat back down in front of the computer.

None of my villagers had any issues with Kan and Lan joining them; in fact, they were very welcoming. Prejudice against beastfolk didn't seem to be a problem in this world.

Dordold introduced Kan and Lan as a married couple, but from their looks alone, I couldn't tell which was male and which was female. The one in red who introduced themself as Lan was *probably* the female.

"These two are excellent carpenters, and they say they can work with stone and metal as well, to a degree. They even used to live in this very cave with the dwarves," Dordold explained.

"We used to live here."

"We learned a lot."

They were even less talkative than Gams. I still wasn't over the fact that my new recruits were more animal than man, and red pandas to boot! I couldn't imagine anything better!

If my memories of the zoo were accurate, red pandas were good at climbing trees. They were omnivorous, too. I knew I couldn't count on that being the case in *The Village of Fate*, though.

The villagers gave Kan and Lan the spare room in the cave. They didn't look like they'd be much help in a fight, but since they were more active at night, they took the role of night watchmen—night watchpandas. If they could lighten Gams's load even a little, that was good enough for me.

A few days passed. Dordold wasn't joking when he said the pandas were good woodworkers. In that time, they'd built a log cabin inside the fence and then moved in to leave the spare room in the cave for storage. Though they were smaller than humans, they were powerful, and their size didn't hinder them. They didn't talk to my villagers a lot, but they looked so cute when they were working that I don't think anyone minded. I took to watching them when there was nothing else to do. But if I seemed too happy, I'd feel a jealous pair of eyes on my back, and I'd have to do something to cheer Destiny up again. I was worried about the pandas' diet at first, but luckily they happily ate whatever the others did.

The peaceful days continued, with the pandas building small structures now and then to help things along. They were currently working on a food storehouse, which would be completed in a few days' time. Kan and Lan even revealed knowledge of a secret storage space within the cave from their time living there before.

In a room full of mining tools and a whole bunch of boards, one of those boards was actually a secret door. The space was only big enough for a child to enter, but Kan climbed in easily and pulled something out.

"This is explosive."

"It's dangerous."

The object was a wooden box with a fuse, like dynamite. Packed inside it were several cylinders.

"Is that a bomb?"

"It's to break bedrock."

"It's dangerous. Don't touch it!" Lan warned, tapping Chem's approaching hand away with a paw.

Despite being scolded, Chem smiled at that soft paw's touch. I watched Kan and Lan curiously as they took the object into their old cave room.

Is that gonna be safe?

Aside from that, the only thing of interest that happened was everyone finding out that Murus was a woman. Though my villagers already knew she was an elf, they hadn't learned her other secret, though Murus didn't seem to be hiding it intentionally. It was thanks to Kan and Lan that everyone found out. Those pandas loved bathing, and so they made a bathtub. Gams thought it would be a great idea to invite all the men in the village to take a bath together, but when he asked Murus, she looked at him in shock.

"I thought you might think I was male, and I suppose you just proved me right."

Murus explained she was female, surprising everybody except Kan, Lan, and Lyra. Apparently, elves didn't take much notice of their gender until they reached a hundred years old, which was when the differences in attitude and speech started to show. If you couldn't tell which gender an elf was by the way they behaved, it was likely you were dealing with a child.

At first, Carol and Chem seemed wary of her, but when they considered that she wasn't particularly feminine—and was more than a hundred years older than Gams—they calmed down. I was the only one who knew how well Murus and Gams got on when they went hunting together. His admirers shouldn't let their guard down so easily.

Interfering with their romantic affairs wouldn't be very god-like of me. I'd just keep a halfhearted eye on things. To be honest, after the stalker incident and asking the villagers for advice with Seika, I was tired of thinking about love stuff for now.

Murus's gender reveal was probably the most impactful thing that happened over the past few days. Apart from that, everything was quiet.

Though my villagers still mainly lived in the cave, with all the extra buildings, it was starting to look like a real village. I was finally playing this game in its intended way.

"We're fine on essentials. It's about time to put some work into the village itself."

Even with Kan and Lan, we still didn't have enough people, and there was only a week until the next Day of Corruption. Still, we had Murus this time, and both Kan and Lan were fighters.

I'd assumed they were weak because of their cuddly appearance, but their strength surprised me. Apparently, it was normal in this world for beastfolk to be stronger than humans, and the pandas used swift movements to confuse their enemies. I witnessed the pandas taking out a monster with Gams—they climbed neatly up a tree with small lances in their mouths and then launched themselves right at their opponent.

We had Gams with his dual swords, Murus with her bow, and Kan and Lan with their lances—a well-balanced team, with Chem as a healer. I didn't know how dangerous the Day of Corruption would be this time around, but if it was like last time, we should be fine. There should be fewer green goblins, too, after our raid on their camp.

But I had to remember that this was still a video game. The difficulty would likely increase steadily over time, and the enemies would get stronger with each battle. I couldn't take anything for granted if I wanted to avoid tragedy. I just wasn't exactly *nervous*. I still had the golem as a trump card, after all.

I had the FP I needed to summon it and a much better idea of how long it could stay active. We dug stakes into the fence just like last time, and my villagers churned up the ground outside the fence to make it harder for enemies to find their footing.

I'd been researching war strategies and traps from the Sengoku era, which I passed on to my villagers via prophecy. Thanks to Kan and Lan and their woodworking skills, recreating the traps was simple.

"I was crapping myself last time, but I just wanna get this

month's Day of Corruption over with." A week was almost too much time to finish up all the preparations.

I leaned back in my chair to stretch and looked over at the tank. My eyes met those of my resident escape artist, who was hanging halfway out of the top.

"C'mon, Destiny. I *just* put you back in there after our walk around the house."

It seemed to hate enclosed spaces, and I let it out to hang around the room with me quite often. I didn't want it wandering and getting into trouble when I was out, though. I needed to teach it to stay in the tank.

It wasn't working.

When it saw my angry gaze, Destiny slipped backwards into the tank like a video on rewind, even nudging the glass lid of its tank back into position. It had mastered the act of escape. It was extremely clever. I would've gladly taken it for a walk if it were warmer, but Sayuki warned me against taking reptiles out into the cold weather. Apparently, they couldn't regulate their internal temperature.

Still, I could imagine Destiny frolicking in the snow, no problem. According to the Internet, there were some resilient lizards in Russia and the Arctic who could survive even the coldest weather, but I wasn't going to risk testing whether Destiny was one of those.

I still didn't know what species it was. Our best guess was an armadillo lizard, but there were so many details that didn't match up that I wasn't convinced.

"I'd love to know what you are, but I guess the most important thing is that we're together."

A mysterious game and a mysterious lizard. Would I ever find out the truth behind either of them? I kept watch over Destiny and the village as I thought, humming with nervous anticipation. While I wanted to know more, a part of me thought it might be better if I stayed ignorant.

THE NPCs IN THIS VILLAGE SIM GAME MUST BE REAL! ↵

chapter 02 A Tough Job and My Endurance

WORK WAS BUSY.

"Everyone's asking for huge end-of-year cleans from us. We're getting into crunch time now, so prepare yourself!"

My boss's words were light, but his expression was serious. I thought I *had* prepared myself...but I didn't even know the half of it.

"Okay, we're done for the morning! Grab some lunch. Then we'll head out to this afternoon's place. After that, we'll hang out in the car until the night shift."

"Yessir."

"Yes, sir..."

My coworkers replied promptly, if unenthusiastically, but I was dead inside. My mind and body were screaming that I couldn't go on.

Before now, a "busy period" at work meant cleaning two places a day, maximum. Each place would never take more than three hours. Lately, however, we cleaned three places most days, sometimes four. Some days, I was at work from before noon until

4 a.m. the next day. I always got a day off following a shift like that, of course, but after several times, my body was reaching its limit. I thought I was ready for some real backbreaking labor, but lately I was getting super close to just calling in sick or something. How did people manage to work from nine to five every day? People must get used to it after a while, but as someone who was new to the working world, it really impressed me. Everyone out there working a full-time job deserves all the praise.

Only my dedication to keeping an eye on my village kept me from completely collapsing. Their circumstances were tougher than mine, and yet they worked hard every single day. There was Carol, who worked unceasingly, despite her small size. Lyra, who was there to keep her family in check and support the entire village. Rodice, who couldn't fight but worked diligently in the background. Chem, who apart from her strange relationship with Gams, represented a perfect pillar of religious hope for the village. Murus, who first came from the Forbidden Forest to monitor the rest of them but now supported them with her skills in archery, pharmacy, and plant-based magic. Then, there was Kan and Lan, who weren't just skilled workers but could put a smile on your face just by watching them.

All it took was a break to watch *The Village of Fate*, and my mood and motivation instantly lifted. What kind of God would I be if I didn't work as hard as they did?

I was grinning at my phone in the minivan as we drove to our next location. Feeling a pair of eyes watching me, I raised my head. Yamamoto-san stared from the seat beside me.

"Wh-what's up?" I asked.

"Is that the game you were talkin' about before?"

Wait, this is bad! I'm not supposed to tell anyone about it, right?

Then again, it wasn't like I was posting about it online. Sayuki had seen it, but I didn't get any letters kicking me out of the game or anything. The company wouldn't know I said anything as long as Yamamoto-san didn't spread it around online. Still, I didn't want to take any risks.

"Uh, yeah. I'm beta-testing it though, so it's not on sale, and I'm not allowed to say anything yet."

"Oh, that's the same with my game, actually. Sucks when you wanna look up strategies online and can't find a damn thing." He seemed more interested in telling me about his game than learning about mine. That suited me just fine.

"I've heard about lawsuits against people sharing information about unreleased games online. Some people had to pay millions of yen, or tens of millions," I said. I hoped he would catch on that I was trying to warn him not to go spreading info about my game, though I was pretty sure he didn't even see the title screen.

"Really? That sounds kind of extreme. Maybe I shouldn't have told you so much about the game I'm playing."

"You only told me it was about capturing territory, but I don't know what it's called. Besides, I'm not going to share it online or tell anyone about it."

"Thanks, I appreciate it. I guess I gotta be more careful. But doesn't it make you wanna talk about it more when you're not allowed to?"

"Oh yeah, I get that a hundred percent." Especially when that game was as amazing as *The Village of Fate*. It wasn't just the game itself; I really wanted to boast about my wonderful villagers and how hard they worked day after day. I was tempted to tell Sayuki about it countless times. I trusted her and didn't think she would rat me out to the company or anything, but I was starting to have my suspicions about the game itself. What if it wasn't just a game? The characters were so humanlike in their behavior, speech, and thoughts. Almost every day I received some parcel full of weird fruit or glowing stones. And then there was Destiny, my mysterious, uncategorizable lizard.

I had a theory, but I had to admit it was a little far-fetched. Some company created a super-complicated A.I., and *The Village of Fate* was the first game to make use of it. They then partnered up with another company that used selective breeding to engineer new fruits and animals. Maybe they were trying to get investors interested, so they could make more money on top of the microtransactions. And wrapped up in this whole stunt was me, an ordinary man.

It was a long shot, but it still made more sense than a game that let me watch a parallel world.

"What's up? You just went quiet."

"I was just thinking. I'm not allowed to tell people about my game either, so I get how you feel."

"It's annoying, right? Still, I trust ya not to spill the beans. You don't seem like much of a gossip."

"Don't worry. I won't tell anyone."

I could let something slip accidentally, but I doubted I would. I was too concerned with my own problems.

"Right, so in this game, you gotta destroy enemy territory, and you pay money to get yourself more monsters. You know the deal. You raise them, they level up by fighting, and you can use items to make them stronger."

A famous example of a game with battling monsters immediately came to mind, but there were a lot of similar ones out there.

"You said you have to capture territory, too, right?" I asked.

"Right, but what makes this game interesting is that you play the villain, and your main objective is to go around destroying villages. The graphics are awesome, too! Oh, and when I say villain, you're actually playing an evil God, and you win the game by destroying all of humanity!"

That was not my kind of thing at all. Besides, I had no time to pick up any new games when I was busy protecting my village.

"The more enemies you kill, the more points you get and the more monsters you can summon. But the microtransactions are kind of insane. You can buy a ton of points with money, so I just end up throwing cash at it all the time."

"Hey, are you me?"

It was like looking in a mirror, though it was hard to find a game nowadays that *didn't* have microtransactions. There was nothing more terrifying than a game without a price tag. I started to wonder how much I'd spent on *The Village of Fate*, but I definitely didn't want to know.

It was worth it, though. I got my money's worth in fruit and meat and all the other offerings. I checked a couple of restaurant prices for boar online, and it was up there. And the fruit was nutritious and tasted amazing—it'd probably be sold as a luxury good if it were on the market.

"You can even increase your territory, but it costs a ton of points. You know, one extra area costs..." Yamamoto-san didn't finish his sentence.

I decided it was safer not to prod him for the exact figure.

"Anyway, I nabbed myself three areas, and two of them got destroyed!"

"What about the latest one? Is that the same one you said got destroyed before?"

"Yeah! Two of my areas got attacked at once. I had to split up my monsters! The less defended area never stood a chance, and one of my strongest and most expensive monsters got killed!" His face twisted up into a smile, but it was empty. "All that money gone just like that."

He seemed distraught, but I'd look the same way—or worse—if my village were destroyed. I wish I knew what to say to cheer him up, but this was where my lack of social skills failed me.

"Well, putting aside the money for a sec, it's a great game. Probably the best I've ever played. I dunno what I'd do if I lost and could never play it again, I bet they're making a ton—"

Just then, the minivan arrived at our next workplace.

"Hey, guys, we gotta get to work, though I'm not gonna say no if you two wanna take a quick nap first," the boss said.

I suddenly realized that the car ride was our whole break, and we used it all up talking. The boss, who had been driving, was going to start working right away. He was older than us; this couldn't be easy on him. We had no right to complain.

"I'm home..."

After an endless day, work was over and I was back at my place. I never did finish up that conversation with Yamamoto-san.

"You look exhausted! Would you like a bath or some dinner first?" Mom offered.

"I'll take the bath..."

I dragged my feet to the bathroom, pulled off my clothes, and slid open the glass door to the wet room...only to find my sister already in the tub.

Mom! Didn't you know she was in here?!

"I didn't realize you were a pervert."

"Look, I'm dead tired. It was an accident."

Sayuki glared at me. I couldn't see anything because of the steam. Just in case, I covered my crotch with my hands. It wasn't a huge deal—we were related.

"Just lemme know when you're out."

Being related didn't mean we were about to bathe together, though. As I turned to leave, I felt hot splashes of water on my back.

"Why don't you just wash, and I'll get out when you're done?" Sayuki suggested.

I didn't mind, but I never expected a suggestion like that to come from her. Maybe I was the weird one for making such a big deal of it. It wasn't too long ago that she complained about having to use the bathroom after me. This was progress. Those thoughts drifted lazily through my half-dead mind as I began to shampoo my hair. I was so exhausted. Even my thoughts were making me tired.

"You still have that scar on your stomach," Sayuki said, resting her jaw on the side of the tub.

"Eek! Stop it, you perv!"

"Very funny. At least put some feeling into it if you're gonna act like a dork."

Everyone's a critic.

"I'm sorry, Oniichan. First, you get stabbed, and then you end up getting into it with that jerk all over again."

Sayuki hadn't sounded so glum in a while. I heard tears in her voice, even if I couldn't see them.

"Don't sweat it. It's a brother's job to protect his sister, and I failed last time."

"No, you didn't. You took the blow for me."

"Only because I froze. I'm sorry you have such a pathetic brother."

I remembered panicking, thinking of nothing but escape as I begged a young Yoshinaga for my life. He was still in junior high school. My memories were hazy due to the injury, but I *did* know I acted like a wimp.

"Sometimes it's like we're not talking about the same thing. Are you sure your memories aren't messed up?" Sayuki asked.

"I was yelling at Yoshinaga, and he got mad and pulled a knife on me. And you said to him, 'If you're gonna stab someone, stab me, but don't lay a finger on my sister!'"

I...didn't remember it like that. Maybe Sayuki made it up to make me feel better. I looked up at her; she was smiling at me with tears rolling down her face.

Is she serious?

Maybe I felt so guilty about failing to protect her that my mind twisted my memories to be worse than the actual event. I knew false memories were a common phenomenon, especially when the event was so long ago. How many of my recollections were real, and how many did I subconsciously fabricate over the past ten years, both for the better and for the worse? I ignored my dad's kindness and painted him as a grumbling obstruction to my happiness. I wasn't just running away from reality but from my past, and it looked like all that running had affected my memories. How could I be so stupid?

"Even then, I didn't save you," I said.

"What d'you mean? After he stabbed you, Yoshinaga ran away! You *did* save me. Though you did look pretty scared!" Sayuki glared at me and splashed me with more bath water.

"Quit it! The water's going up my nose!" I grabbed the shower head and doused her with the cold water as revenge.

"That's freezing!" Sayuki screeched. "I'm mad now!"

"Hey, I was *already* mad!"

Sayuki had a bucket in hand as I armed myself with the showerhead.

"Stop using the bathroom as a playground! How old are you two?!"

Mom's angry shout forced us into a ceasefire.

chapter 03 The Village's Daily Life and My Daily Life

T HE NEXT DAY was my first off work in a while. I planned to sleep until lunchtime and be lazy all day, but I woke with the morning sun and was sitting at my PC before I knew it. I'd been working so much lately that I always had to watch my villagers on my phone, and it felt nice to sit down and take my time with them. My villagers were already hard at work, despite the early hour. Well, all but three of them.

Carol was still fast asleep in her bed. Kan and Lan were nocturnal, and at this hour they were snuggled up together in their cabin. If Rodice and Lyra cuddled like that, I'd look away, but with pandas I couldn't see it as anything but adorable. It was tempting just to watch them till they woke up, but I knew I should check on the others.

Chem and Lyra were preparing breakfast. Thanks to the new ingredients and seasonings, their meals had been more varied lately. That made everyone happy.

"It's a chilly day! Why don't we make a nice warm soup?" Lyra suggested.

"What a wonderful idea! I'm sure Gams must be freezing, too."

The women kept working as they chatted. They made eight portions, even if Kan and Lan wouldn't be ready to eat for a while. Even with the increase in population, Chem and Lyra still cooked for everyone, and they were getting really good at it.

Chem started setting the table with an occasional glance outside toward the watchtower, where Gams was keeping watch. The winter cold was bad enough, but the wind atop the tower was chilling. Gams had several pelts with him up there, wrapped tightly around his shoulders. He stared out over the fence and into the wide forest that stretched out beyond it. Kan or Lan usually took the night watch, and they fared better since their thick fur naturally protected them against the cold. Gams had no such fur, and recently I learned that he really hated the cold. He wrapped himself up in a cocoon, leaving only his face uncovered. It looked a little silly, but it was sweet, too.

He never complained. That wasn't a luxury he could have so close to the Day of Corruption. My villagers were ready for it, but he knew firsthand how dangerous it would be. No wonder he was on high alert as the day came closer.

As Gams kept watch in his bundle of furs, a figure approached him from behind.

"Thank you for keeping watch when it's so cold. I brought you a warm drink, and it's almost time for breakfast."

"Thanks." Gams took the wooden cup from Murus with both hands to warm them.

Murus smiled and sat beside him. "How is the monster situation?"

"There aren't as many green goblins this time, since we destroyed their camp."

They did that for Murus's sake, but everyone benefited from it. If we were lucky, there wouldn't be *any* green goblins on the Day of Corruption, either.

"I shall never be able to thank you enough for that."

"Hey, you're one of us now. You don't need to thank us. You're family."

"Family...that sounds nice," Murus murmured, leaning against Gams.

No way...

They seemed to be getting on *very* well. No matter how much Carol and Chem fawned over Gams, they were both in situations which would make a relationship inappropriate. Gams and Murus had a significant age gap, too, but in a much safer direction.

I was a little jealous Gams got all that attention, but I understood why. He took on twice as much responsibility as everyone else; he deserved nice things in his life.

"That's it, Gams! Put your arm around her!"

As though he heard me, Gams rearranged his blankets to let Murus in underneath. I watched the pair with bated breath as they looked into each other's eyes.

"You were cold, right? I'm sorry I didn't notice," said Gams.

What the hell, Gams?!

Her cheeks a little red, Murus responded with an awkward smile.

I've seen smoother protagonists in dating sims, for God's sake!

If he'd played his cards right, he could've gotten kissed right then and there. He was completely hopeless! As his God, I was very disappointed in him.

I guess I already knew he wasn't great with relationships. He didn't seem to notice the more extreme aspects of his sister's affections, nor see Carol's love as anything more than a kid looking up to him. At first I thought he was being tactful, but now I realized he was just clueless.

"I guess it's okay if he's a bit dense. Getting into a relationship with Murus would only spell trouble."

I was half joking, but the scenario that played out in my mind was far from funny. Two assassins with blades in hand, following Gams and Murus wherever they went. I wished I didn't believe it was possible.

As their God, I decided not to interfere.

The other human man of the village, Rodice, was making notes on their transactions with Dordold. The village had made more than they'd expected, and most of that money would go into developing it further. The villagers had also bought new clothes, and they were wearing outfits I hadn't seen before. Though the men didn't care so much, the women were very excited. They didn't even care that their laundry load increased.

Lyra and Chem were wearing new clothes that seemed easier to move in than their old outfits. After seeing them in the same outfits for weeks on end, seeing them in new clothes was refreshing. Chem dashed outside once breakfast was ready. She glared up at the watchtower like she could sense a disturbance in the force.

"Gams! Breakfast is ready! And have you seen Murus?"

"On my way! Murus is with me!"

"What? Up there?" Chem was doing a bad job of sounding surprised, the frown not leaving her face.

"Gams!" Carol stood beside Chem, a stuffed animal in her arms.

The villagers had bought the teddy bear from Dordold along with the clothes. When did Carol get there, anyway? I could swear she popped up out of nowhere. I was sometimes jealous of those anime protagonists always surrounded by girls, but seeing what Gams dealt with cured me of that envy.

"Reality can be so disappointing..."

Gams climbed down from the watchtower, and Chem and Carol moved to flank him. They each grabbed one of his hands and pulled him towards the cave. Murus watched them go with a gentle smile on her face. Maybe it was the wisdom of age that kept her from being jealous. Or were her feelings towards Gams just not romantic?

I'd never been in a relationship in my life; I couldn't make a proper judgment. I shouldn't read into it too deeply.

Everyone aside from Kan and Lan sat down for a breakfast of soup, fried meat, and vegetables, with some rice-like corn substance—more stuff that they bought from Dordold. It looked heavy for breakfast, but that made sense when you had a day of labor ahead. Plus, they had a ton of meat, just like we did at home. The meat they sent us after the last Day of Corruption was still taking up more than half our fridge and freezer space. I was willing to bet there'd be meat for dinner tonight, not that I was complaining. It was so delicious I doubted I'd ever get tired of it—and it went with everything.

After breakfast, my villagers took a short break, as they often did. Only Gams immediately went back to his post on the watchtower.

"Now's my chance."

I went downstairs to eat my own breakfast and use the bathroom before returning to the PC. When I got back, the sun had begun to rise, and Lyra, Chem, and Carol had started their chores. Murus and Gams had left the village to explore and gather food. Though my villagers had plenty of rations to last the winter, it never hurt to have more, and they could store whatever they couldn't eat. Rodice was on watch from the tower now, having taken over from Gams.

They'd picked up a flute in Murus's village. The person on watch would blow it if they caught sight of any monsters, and it was loud enough that Gams and Murus could hear it when they were out.

The morning passed peacefully, and it was soon lunchtime. Today my villagers ate at a table outside, as they often did when the day was clear. This time, Kan and Lan joined them. I ate my cup ramen and fruit along with everyone.

"Oh, right! I forgot about you." I glanced at Destiny.

The lizard often joined me in front of the PC. No matter how carefully I put on the tank lid, Destiny always managed to escape. I passed it some fruit. It took it and ate with both hands.

"Wanna keep an eye on the village with me?"

After lunch, I sat back and played lazily with Destiny as we watched the PC. The villagers started work again for the afternoon. Murus was on the watchtower. Kan and Lan were shaving down logs to make some simple furniture. Gams and Rodice were out collecting lumber, while Lyra, Chem, and Carol were collecting herbs and edible plants together.

"That reminds me. They sent me a mix of those healing herbs in a tube, but I have no idea if they work or not."

The herbs arrived three days ago, a liquid mix of Murus's own making, stored in a pinky-sized wooden tube since glass was rare in their world. When I opened the top, a strong herbal smell was released. I poured a tiny drop on my desk and found a pale green liquid with the same consistency as water.

Everything the village had sent me so far was healthy, so I doubted this was dangerous. In fact, it would probably end up being the most effective medicine in existence. Heh. Maybe that was optimistic.

My villagers mentioned that the herbs were for treating wounds; maybe I could use it if I cut myself. Then again, I didn't want to be the guinea pig for an unknown medicine. But I also didn't want to reject a gift from my villagers, so I decided to treat it as a good luck charm for now.

I lifted some weights as I watched the village, and before I knew it, it was getting dark. Mom called me for dinner just as my villagers were preparing theirs. I put Destiny back in the tank and headed downstairs. Today, it was just me and Mom.

"They're working late tonight, huh?"

"Things are busy for both of them right now."

Guess it's not just the cleaning industry that suffers this time of year...

As we ate, Mom talked my ear off about this and that. I used to mostly ignore her, since she would always ask when I was going to get a job, but nowadays I listened and nodded at all the right moments. Rodice's family, Gams, and Chem all taught me how important it was to keep family relationships peaceful.

After dinner I had a bath and then returned to my room. My computer screen was still bright. Living in the cave wasn't just safer, but it also meant they had lights at night. They stayed up a little later than they had before, though they still had an earlier bedtime than most people in the real world. Everyone other than Kan and Lan would soon be asleep. One of the pandas would keep watch on the tower while the other continued with their woodworking projects.

"I should probably hit the sack, too. I have an early start tomorrow."

Thanks to *The Village of Fate*, I had developed a healthier lifestyle. It was a peaceful, stable game, but somehow it was still extremely satisfying to play. It wouldn't be everyone's cup of tea, but I loved it. Today, as ever, *The Village of Fate* filled me with the motivation I needed to work hard.

"Good night. See you guys tomorrow," I said to my PC, before settling into my futon and closing my eyes.

chapter 04 — Changes in People and Changes in Me

"**T**HREE MORE DAYS."

My mind wandered to the Day of Corruption as I cleaned the corridor of a multi-story building. Last time, the event started around lunchtime and ended in the evening. Knowing the timing was reassuring. We now had Murus, Kan, and Lan with us; our fighting power had increased fourfold. Even if the game ramped up the difficulty, we'd be prepared for it.

"I can tell you're gettin' distracted!" called my boss.

I immediately straightened up. Right, I needed to focus on my work.

"So—"

"Sorry!"

Before I could finish my apology, Yamamoto-san cut me off and bowed his head.

Oh. He wasn't talking to me.

A large pile of dirt sat at Yamamoto-san's feet. He must have knocked over the nearby potted plant by accident.

"What's up, Yama? You're always lookin' so sleepy lately. You can take a day off if you need to, y'know," said the boss.

"I'm fine. Just need to go to bed earlier. I can't really afford to take a day off..." Yamamoto-san replied listlessly.

The boss wasn't the only one who noticed his behavior. Even when we had a break or traveled by car, Yamamoto-san didn't nap. Instead, he'd play on his phone, the light illuminating the tired hollows of his face. He used to talk to me, but now he was absolutely focused on his game. He seemed to be having some trouble. He'd never let the game get in the way of his work ethic before.

Yamamoto-san worked the rest of the day with his head in the clouds. I couldn't stop thinking about him even as I bought my usual drink at the convenience store. He'd been acting strange for a few days now. I was obsessed with my own game but not to the same extent. Occasionally, I saw him frowning at the screen and desperately hitting buttons.

A few days ago, he shared something with me, catching me totally off guard. I promised him I would keep it a secret.

"The game I'm playing has a reward system. Remember I said you could get points for destroying villages and camps? You can change those points into real money. Hard to believe, huh?"

"You're kidding, right? I've never heard of a game doing that."

We were talking about games during our break when Yamamoto-san came out with that shocking revelation. I thought it was only streamers and pro gamers who could make money off of playing.

"I didn't think you'd believe me at first. I didn't either, so I destroyed this one place as a test and converted the points I got... and then money showed up in my bank account just like that."

And here I thought *The Village of Fate* was innovative for sending me random gifts. I wouldn't have believed him if my own game wasn't so out of the ordinary. My game might even be stranger.

"It wasn't just a couple hundred yen either," Yamamoto-san continued, his voice low.

He didn't look like he was joking. Just how much did he make off this game?

"It's an online game, by the way, so there's gotta be other people playing it. There was this huge village that other players were already attacking. I showed up when it was barely hanging on. I destroyed it and snatched the victory."

That reminded me of an old online game I used to play, where weaker guilds would team up to siege the castles of stronger guilds. Other guilds would jump in at the last minute to steal the final blow and claim the castle for themselves.

"If the money was bad, I wouldn't be playin' this as seriously as I am..." Yamamoto-san trailed off and looked around, as though he wasn't sure whether to continue.

What? It was just getting interesting!

"How much did you get exactly?" I asked.

"Promise me you won't tell anyone, okay? It was...five million yen."

"Five mi—" I quickly clapped my hands over my mouth.

"That's big money, right? Look, I don't really like to whine about my situation, but my family ain't exactly well off. My old man disappeared and left us with his debt, so I had to drop outta high school to start working. Just when I thought it was all paid off, Mom got involved with another guy who...ran away and left his debt behind," he explained.

I wanted to offer comfort, but I couldn't think of anything. While I was busy doing nothing in my room for years on end, Yamamoto-san was working hard to pay off a debt he shouldn't be responsible for. What could I say to someone like that? Even just something like "that's too bad" sounded rude. I just listened in silence.

"People told me that I shouldn't bother paying the money back, but scumbag or not, he's my dad, y'know? Even if he borrowed all that money, it was money that went into raising me. Pretending it's got nothing to do with me would make me feel gross. Plus, I spent my best teenage years and my twenties paying it all off. I didn't get to party like other people my age. I don't wanna start ignoring that debt now, 'cause it'll make all the time I spent working pointless."

Legally speaking, a child had no responsibility for their parents' debt, and I agreed with that. It wasn't Yamamoto-san's fault his dad got into debt, after all. I did admire his integrity, at least. It put him at a disadvantage, but it was honorable.

"Anyway, that's why I was super grateful to have this game as extra income. I even paid back most of Mom's debt from it. I've got no skills and no qualifications. This game might be the only chance I have to turn my life around." Determination burned in Yamamoto's eyes.

He frightened me a little, to tell the truth.

We finished ahead of schedule, but it was still dark by the time we were done. It wasn't that late, but the sun set so early in winter. My way home was lit only by a few streetlights and the lights from the homes along the road. It made the early dark even more obvious.

"Poor Yamamoto-san..." I muttered to myself as I walked.

He didn't tell me much about his game, but he treated it like a second job. The game paid better than the cleaning work, and he might be better off doing it full-time. Then again, betting your entire life on a video game was reckless.

We were due to finish up work for the year tomorrow and wouldn't be starting again until January 5th. I just hoped Yamamoto-san got some rest over the break. It wasn't my place to worry, but he was the coworker I got on best with. I cared about his well-being.

I carried on, thoughts of Yamamoto-san and the village swirling in my mind until the lights of my house came into view. I'd walked so slowly that my body was chilled to its core. Eager to warm myself up, I jumped into the house and pulled off my shoes before heading to the living room. It looked like I just missed dinner.

"Welcome back, Yoshio," said my mom. "Have you eaten?"

"Nope."

"I'll heat something up for you."

Mom went into the kitchen, and I crouched in front of the electric heater, silently praising whoever invented this thing.

"Quit hogging the heater!" Sayuki sat down next to me, trying to push me out of the way.

I wasn't about to let her steal my precious warmth. We struggled for the prime spot in front of the heater.

"Ugh. You're too strong! Oh, hey, what are your plans for New Year's? Are you gonna come with us to see Granddad?"

I'd forgotten about that. At the end of every year, my family always went to my dad's childhood home, but the last time I went with them was ten years ago. They wouldn't come back till January 4th, giving me a few peaceful days to spend holed up in the house.

"You can come this year, can't you?" Dad asked, not turning around from his spot on the sofa.

I got the subtext. I could come this year because I finally had a job and didn't need to be ashamed to face my grandparents. I loved them, and of course I wanted to see them again—but the Day of Corruption was coming up, and work had told me they might need to call me in on short notice. The boss might even call me before he called Yamamoto-san, with how late he'd been recently.

"I'd love to go, but I've got work. Can you tell them I'll come see them another time?"

"Aww. That's a shame, but I guess it can't be helped."

"It doesn't have to be New Year's for us to go see them. Make sure you can come with us next time, Yoshio," Mom said kindly.

Meanwhile, Sayuki glared at me. Didn't she like going to see our grandparents?

"Guess I'll stay home this year, too," she said.

"I thought you were looking forward to going to the shrine and seeing Grandma and Granddad?" asked Mom.

"Well, yeah, but..."

"You should go," I said. "Make sure you bring me back some treats."

I didn't want her to stay home on my account.

"Okay. I'll go," Sayuki said with a sigh.

I didn't get why she sounded so down about it. The age gap between us made her hard to understand sometimes.

After eating, I went back upstairs and watched my villagers sleep, going over my plans for the next few days.

My family was due to leave at around midday tomorrow, and I'd have my last work shift for the year. I felt a sad prick in my chest as I realized no one would be there to welcome me home afterward.

I had plenty of food, at least. Every year, Mom made a special array of dishes to celebrate the new year, and she set aside some for me to have at home. The fridge was still stocked with food from *The Village of Fate*, and since I hadn't bought any FP in a while, I had money from work if I needed anything more. I also had more cooking skills than before.

I wonder if there are any in-game events to mark the new year?

Some online games ran campaigns to reward their players during this season. I checked through the game's options and backlog, but didn't see anything like that.

"Doesn't look like I can roll the egg gacha either, since it's been less than a month."

That was a once-a-month event, but I wasn't sure when it reset. I was super lucky to get Destiny last time; I didn't expect much from my next roll. I should probably let my villagers know not to send me anything around the Day of Corruption.

"I don't wanna have to worry about anything except work tomorrow. After that, it'll be the Day of Corruption, and..." A yawn interrupted my thoughts. "Man, I can't keep my eyes open anymore. Good night, everyone."

With nothing of note happening in my village, I decided to go to bed for the night. But just as I was about to get into my futon, I caught sight of Destiny staring at me from its tank.

"Ah, sorry, I forgot. Good night, Destiny."

Destiny nodded in response.

chapter 05 The End of Work and My Loneliness

"GOOD WORK TODAY! See you next year!"

"Bye! Happy New Year!"

"See you."

The boss and Misaki-san were all smiles as they said goodbye after work, the busy season finally over. Yamamoto-san's goodbye was stiff and quiet.

I got out of the minivan, turned, and bowed my head. "Thank you. Happy New Year! See you guys next year!"

That was exhausting, but I made it. As always, I asked the boss to drop me off outside the convenience store. Since there was no one at home, I decided to stock up on drinks and snacks before heading back. I'd grab some cup ramen, too, just in case.

I waved at the retreating van until it was completely out of sight. Work was over for the year, but I didn't feel much relief. Yamamoto-san's low spirits were weighing on my mind.

He hadn't been himself these past few shifts. He had dark circles under his eyes and grew more and more irritable by the day. I was worried about his mood, but the angry spark in his eyes bothered me more. I felt it seek me out several times as we worked. Whenever I turned, he would look away, but not before I caught a glimpse of his rage. What did I do to make him hate me so much? Maybe something unconscious. I wasn't as good at the work as he was, and I tended to slow everything down.

I tried to get him to talk to me, but he avoided my attempts, and I never got the chance. I wasn't certain, but I think that behavior began the day he caught a glimpse of *The Village of Fate* on my phone.

"Did that have something to do with it?" My question turned into white mist, diffusing into the night.

I kept my eyes on the dark sky, my mind ambling through the possibilities. I couldn't shake the feeling that *The Village of Fate* and whatever game Yamamoto-san was playing were linked somehow. They sounded so similar. They were both in beta, and both of us were forbidden from talking about them. Both relied heavily on microtransactions.

His game's objective was to destroy villages, which was the exact opposite of a village-building sim. That might have been why I didn't pick up on the similarities earlier. Yamamoto-san said he got points for destroying villages, and he also mentioned that one of his territories was recently taken down. I was dumb, but even I could connect the dots.

He destroyed Murus's village. I destroyed the green goblins' camp, his territory. The timing of it all made perfect sense. Yamamoto-san realized it all before I did, which led to his change in attitude. It all added up.

The Village of Fate was an online game—it wasn't strange to find out that other people were involved. In fact, it would be stranger if it was single player. I was so distracted by the overly complex A.I. and systems of my game that I barely gave Yamamoto-san's a second thought. But if my theory was correct, his game put him in direct competition with *The Village of Fate*.

"I bet we're not the only players, either."

The lore of the game contained several other Minor Gods. Each one of them must be a player. Then there were the Corrupted Gods like the one Yamamoto-san controlled. The two sides collided within the game world. If I was dealing with real human opponents, I needed to change up my strategy.

"I guess it makes stuff more interesting, but I don't like having to fight Yamamoto-san."

If he really was mad at me for destroying his territory, then we couldn't fix this with a simple conversation. We weren't even permitted to talk about our games. It didn't matter now, with the cat out of the bag, but I couldn't go posting around online to see if anyone else was playing.

"But the company would never know if we spoke about it face-to-face, right?"

Then again, this game was so full of surprises, I couldn't be sure. The one thing I wanted to avoid at all costs was losing my villagers.

This was clearly more than just a game. Yamamoto-san was earning serious money. The stakes were too high for this to be cleared up in a single talk.

"Maybe I should just stay away from him for a while."

Without coming to a clear conclusion, I made it home. I announced my homecoming out of habit, but of course no one was there to welcome me.

Or so I thought.

"Welcome back!"

"Huh?"

Who was that? I knew it was a female voice, but I didn't recognize it. Hadn't my family left yet? Maybe Dad had to finish up something urgent for work.

"Are you guys still here?" I pushed open the living room door and looked around.

There was a woman cooking in the attached kitchen, her back to me.

"Dinner'll be ready in a sec."

"What are you doing here?"

The woman turned around, wiping her steamed-up glasses with her fingers. It was Seika, wearing an apron.

"What? Did no one tell you? Your mom asked me to cook for you."

"Mom... Why?"

Mom got on well with Seika. She probably realized we were starting to talk again and wanted to "help."

"Well, thanks for cooking, but what about your grandma?"

"She went back to her hometown for the new year. Usually I go with her, but I can't this year because of my foot. It's basically healed, but the doctor said I shouldn't push myself yet." Her cast was gone, and she'd stopped using crutches a while ago. "I don't like eating by myself. Mind if we eat together?"

"Sounds good! I'd prefer not to eat alone either."

Before we fell out of touch, we used to eat together almost every day. Eating with her was big on its own, but I hadn't seen her wearing an apron in years. I smiled, wondering if this was what married life was like.

Hang on, I'm getting ahead of myself...

Seika was a kind soul through and through, and we were always as close as family. Despite all my failings, she was still here to take care of me. Maybe she considered this a chore, but that was okay. Right now, I was lucky just to talk to her—all thanks to my villagers' advice. Asking for more would be selfish.

"So, what's for—"

As I approached the kitchen, I spotted Destiny sitting on the floor, looking up at Seika. Seika hated reptiles; if she spotted it, she'd freak out! I dived towards it and scooped it up, hiding it cradled in my arms.

"Wh-what're you doing?" Seika asked. "You'll make me burn myself!"

"I was just, uh, picking up something that fell from the shelf. I didn't want you to step on it." I turned my back to her and hurried Destiny back to my room.

I made sure the door was properly closed before setting the lizard down on my desk.

"You gave me a heart attack! Please behave, okay? Seika's not a huge fan of reptiles." I clasped my hands together.

Destiny blinked at me and scratched its head. Even if it didn't understand, it would usually at least nod. I couldn't shake the feeling it was playing dumb on purpose.

"If you stay here, I'll give you double the normal amount for dinner. I'll even throw in a bunch of fruit. Whaddya say?"

There was a pause. Finally, Destiny nodded and held out its hand. I placed my index finger in its palm, which it grabbed strongly, and we shook on it.

"Are you sure you don't understand what I'm saying?"

It flicked its tongue in and out nonchalantly.

Is it...doing this on purpose?

"Whatever. Y'know, I thought it'd be just you and me for New Year's."

Destiny was the other reason I didn't accompany my parents to the countryside. I couldn't leave it here by itself. I offered to look after Sayuki's reptile, too, but apparently it was hibernating and didn't need any care right now.

"Dinner's ready!"

"Coming!"

I glanced at the tank and spotted the remains of some fruit. Someone must've fed Destiny before they left at lunchtime.

"Don't forget our promise. I'll bring you the tastiest cut of meat, too."

Destiny shifted the lid of its tank and crawled back inside obediently. I decided not to put too much thought into its behavior.

I hurried downstairs and sat at the dinner table, feeling bad for not helping Seika with anything. I could've at least set the table. Well, I'd help with the washing up after.

"I just used some of the meat you had in the fridge..."

"It's fine. You can use whatever. You can even take some stuff home with you if you want."

"Oh, it's okay. Your mom's already passing stuff on to us when she has too much."

Last I heard, we were getting so many offerings that Mom was making the rounds handing the extra stuff out to neighbors, and yet our fridge was still packed.

"This meat really is good! It's delicious, and it wakes me right up after a tiring day at work. It seems like Obaachan gets her energy back after eating this stuff, too."

Okiku-baachan worked in the fields every day. She also did papercut art, ceramics, and handicrafts during the week. If she had enough energy for all of that before, I could only imagine what the meat did for her.

"She hasn't changed in ten years, huh?"

I didn't know how old she was, but she looked the same as she did when I was in college. Maybe even since I was a kid.

"She won't even tell me how old she is!" Seika exclaimed. "How's it taste?"

"Delicious, just like everything you make. Especially the miso soup. It's super refreshing. Think you could teach Sayuki how to cook?"

Seika laughed. "Thanks! Sayuki-chan's getting way better, you know. She came around to my place, and I taught her a couple of dishes. Her omelets are pretty good now!"

This was the first I'd heard of it. Sayuki was always so bad at cooking that I was in charge of the food whenever our parents were out.

Seika and I chatted some more, did the dishes, and then I walked her home.

"Can I swing by again tomorrow?" she asked.

"Sure, but just make sure you're not pushing yourself. Only come if you're super bored."

"I've got so much spare time, I don't know what to do with it! I'll come round, and we can have soba to ring in the new year!"

Seika closed the door behind her, leaving me alone once again.

"Ringing in the new year together, huh?"

That suggestion made my heart leap. What was I, a teenager?

When I was a student, I always imagined adults spent their nights drinking at fancy bars and picking up women. Now that ten years had passed, I realized I hadn't grown up as much as I thought.

Ten years, huh?

What a long time to do absolutely nothing valuable with my life. I was better at talking to girls back when I was a student. I was so emotionally immature.

I wasn't good enough to be Seika's boyfriend. That wasn't what I was after. I had no right to ask for more from her.

I sat down in the fragrant bathwater, trying to rid myself of the negative thoughts.

"Baths are great for healing the body and the mind, huh? This is—"

I cut myself off with a yelp. Just when I was beginning to relax, I remembered something and jumped out of the bath. Pulling my clothes back over my damp body, I raced upstairs to my room.

Destiny was glaring at me, sitting on my desk with its arms folded. I fell to my knees and apologized earnestly before preparing it the most lavish feast I'd ever made.

THE NPCs IN THIS VILLAGE SIM GAME MUST BE REAL! ↵

chapter 06
The Day of Corruption and My Second Foolish Idea

STRETCHED OUT in the morning sunlight and ate a leisurely breakfast. Today was the Day of Corruption.

Seika's not due to come over till the evening, so I've got the whole day to focus on my village!

Hopefully, I could wrap everything up before she arrived. Last time I had no idea when the event would start, and I was on edge the moment the clock struck midnight. In the end, it didn't start until the afternoon, and there was a siren-like sound and a flashing notification to announce the event's start. I wouldn't be caught off guard today, but that didn't mean I was going to completely relax.

I had the app open on my phone during breakfast, just in case something happened. Once I'd eaten, I collected snacks, fruit, and drinks for my lunch and took them back to my room with me. Destiny was sitting on my desk like it was the most natural thing in the world, but I wasn't going to tell it off today.

"Let's get through this together."

Destiny took the fruit I passed over and began to chew, nodding. It was still two hours until midday, but I wanted to see what my villagers were up to.

Just like in real life, the skies in *The Village of Fate* were clear today. I was worried about the risk of snow, but for now, the watchtower's view was unobstructed. At the moment, Murus was up there. Elves had better eyes than humans, and her bow could pick off enemies from a distance, making her the best choice for the job. Before, it was always Gams on the watchtower, and occasionally Rodice, but seeing him trembling up there always made me nervous.

I was glad that Murus was here to take the pressure off the two men and glad for the extra fighting power Kan and Lan brought to the village, although they were asleep right now. They were up until sunrise keeping watch, so they deserved a rest.

Gams was spending his time quietly in the cave. He offered to keep watch with Murus, but the others forced him to take a break. He needed to be fighting fit when the monsters arrived. I agreed that he should rest for now.

Rodice's family sat chatting together, acting like it was a regular day to keep Carol from getting scared. Chem had been polishing my statue since the morning, keeping herself busy by sorting offerings and cleaning. She must have been doing everything she could to hold off her nerves, a feeling I understood. I was trying to tell myself I was calm, but I couldn't stop fidgeting. Destiny stared at the computer screen with the same intensity as me, the fruit still grasped in its hands.

"Wonder what it's thinking."

Destiny came from *The Village of Fate*. Lore-wise, that was its home. I knew it was just a fantasy, but if Destiny really had come from that world, then maybe it wanted to go back. I glanced at it, feeling a prick of anxiety in my chest at the serious glint in its eyes. Even if that world did exist, I had no way to send Destiny back. I gently stroked the top of its head with a finger. It narrowed its eyes in pleasure.

The afternoon came around without incident, until the alarm started blaring from my PC.

"The Day of Corruption is here!"

The same red letters as last time appeared on the screen. I took a deep breath and prepared myself for what lay ahead. I was way more ready than last month, but I didn't know what to expect. If Yamamoto-san was somehow involved, I needed to brace for a more aggressive attack this time around.

Assuming that my opponent was a player... No, I had to assume it was a *specific* player. I needed to plan my strategy as though I was facing Yamamoto-san, that *he* was the one targeting my village. I could sort out the messy emotional stuff once we got through the day. I just needed to focus right now.

Murus spotted something in the distance and blew on the flute, drawing Gams and the others from the cave.

"We've got five direwolves and five boarnabies approaching!" Murus called down before firing her bow.

She hit one of the wolves squarely in the head, but the rest were already at the fence.

"Look after the others, Chem!" Gams said.

"Of course! Come on, everyone! Into the cave!"

Chem took Rodice's family back inside and closed the door. A peephole allowed them to keep an eye on what was happening outside.

Gams, Murus, Kan, and Lan were all out there on defense. Four fighters were so much better than one.

One of the boarnabies charged the fence but then vanished seconds before reaching it, falling into one of the pit traps and impaling itself on the sharpened wooden stakes at the bottom. Its body twitched grotesquely as it died, and I had to remind myself this was all for the villagers' survival.

The wolves didn't need to worry about the pit traps. Just like last time, they made to leap over the fence. Two of them were shot down in midair by Murus, and the two that made it over died instantly at the hands of Gams, Kan, and Lan.

"This is perfect."

My villagers dispatched every monster without a hitch, their plans working flawlessly. I checked the map to make sure nothing lay in hiding, but everything was quiet. I couldn't see into the forest, but the land around the fence had been cleared, so I could see any monsters before they got too close. Since Murus didn't spot any more when she was on the watchtower, we should be safe.

My fighters left the confines of the fence to collect the pig bodies from the pit traps. They then camouflaged the hole again with a thin plank, earth, and dead leaves. If my opponent had as much control over his monsters as I did my villagers, the trap would work, but we'd be out of luck if he could control them directly. Though I doubted he could control ten of them at once.

The way the monsters behaved led me to believe they were acting mostly on instinct, and all the times I spotted Yamamoto-san frowning at his phone, I never saw him tapping on the screen. Although, that was assuming he was my opponent at all. I could still be wrong.

Even if we had an easy start, I was prepared for the worst-case scenario. I couldn't let myself get caught up in guilt or anger and risk my village.

Exactly thirty minutes after the first attack, the second one came. An identical group of monsters, the scenario playing out in exactly the same way.

"Maybe they're just computer controlled? Or maybe my opponent dictates their attack patterns in advance, and then they're set in stone?"

If it was like the daily prophecy, perhaps he could pick the target and the monsters to attack once a day but couldn't control it more than that. There could be a limit to how many monsters he could dispatch at a time, which would mean we wouldn't be seeing more than ten at once. If that was the case, this would be easy. My village would see this through no problem.

Then came the next three attacks. Surprisingly, each had one monster fewer than the attack before it. Thirty minutes after the fifth, there was nothing.

"Wait, it was like this last time, too. Sometimes we got an hour between attacks, but the attacks that came after a longer break had more monsters in them."

The next wave would be bigger. I used the chance to take a bathroom break and wash my face, refreshing myself. I then shared some fruit with Destiny, and together we waited for the next attack.

The last attack was an hour ago, and yet nothing was happening.

"What's going on?"

Just like that, the pattern I expected was broken.

I've got a bad feeling about this...

Two more hours passed, and the sun began to set. We were coming up on the time of the final wave last month. Was the enemy planning to send all his monsters in at once? That was a good strategy. Even if he could buy more points with money, his choices were limited. If he knew I only had four fighters, pouring everything he had into a single attack to overwhelm me was the right choice. "Strength in numbers," as a wise tactician once said... a wise tactician in one of my manga.

Maybe Yamamato-san had just...run out of money, since he had complained about how much he spent on the game before. He might be out of the points he needed to summon the monsters.

I checked the time. Just over ten minutes left.

"Once we're through this, maybe I'll try and give him a call."

Great, but what am I supposed to say to him? Won't he think I'm calling him just to brag?

Or maybe I'd find out I was wrong all along, which would be fine by me.

"I really hope my real-life problems and my in-game problems stay separate..." I leaned back in my chair and looked up at the ceiling. This game made my life better. By that logic, it also had the power to make my life worse.

"I guess everything's got its bad points, whether it's a video game, or...huh?"

I heard a noise from downstairs. Was Seika here already?

Dammit, the Day of Corruption was dragging on longer than I thought. Out here in the sticks, we only locked our doors at night, so Seika must have just come in. Since my room was on the second floor, I didn't always hear the doorbell when it rang, especially if I was focused on something.

I'd ask her for some time to wrap this up. I rushed downstairs.

"You're early! I'm kinda busy with something, d'you mind waiting for a little bit?"

There was no reply, but I heard movement from the living room. I went in and found a man dressed entirely in black. Not only were his clothes jet black, but he was wearing a balaclava and holding a crowbar. Having expected Seika, I could do nothing but stand and stare in shock.

Somehow, I managed to suppress my scream. I found myself saying something surprising instead.

"Yamamoto-san?"

part 8

DESTRUCTION

AND A VISITOR ↵

THE NPCs IN THIS VILLAGE SIM GAME MUST BE REAL! ↵

chapter 01 Yamamoto's World

S OMEONE NEW showed up today.

Two men stepped out of the car. The first was around the same age as the boss and looked like he rarely cracked a smile. He spoke to the boss like they were old friends. The other guy just stood there. He was tall and well built. His face was sickly pale, and for some reason he was wearing a tracksuit. His behavior was odd. He wouldn't meet anyone's gaze at all, and he kept bobbing his head up and down like a woodpecker. He must have been somewhere around my age.

From the sound of it, the older man was friends with the boss, and his son was...troubled. Apparently, he suffered from depression and had poor social skills. I immediately understood. The boss was being "helpful" again; trying to save someone who needed it but didn't necessarily want it. Someone like me.

"I-I'll do my best." The man bent himself over in a ninety-degree bow.

He looked serious enough, but it was possible he wouldn't make it more than a few shifts. As the one teaching him the ropes, I hoped he'd pull through.

He worked harder than I expected. We only had him on the basic machinery, but he worked diligently without complaint. He wasn't great at the job, but at least he wasn't awful. I knew cleaning companies had a bad rep among people looking for part-time work, but this guy didn't seem to think badly of us. He was super eager to do his job and listened seriously to the tips I gave him. I wanted to have high hopes for him, but he wouldn't be the first to show promise on his first day only to ghost us after.

"Still at it, huh?" I said, seeing Yoshio working hard again.

I really thought he'd throw in the towel, but he came back every time and gave it his all. Not only that, but we had a lot in common, despite my initial assessment he'd be too serious. Turned out he was a gamer like me, so we had a lot to talk about during our breaks. We had different tastes in genres, but it was still great to have a coworker to talk to. The boss was an outdoorsy type, while Misaki-san preferred reading to gaming. I finally had something to look forward to during my breaks.

Yoshio told me he used to be a shut-in and hadn't worked in the ten years since he graduated college. It caught me by surprise. I knew people like him were common these days, but I felt a little weird about it.

I was forced to quit high school for the sake of my family, but this guy had the luxury of choice. And he wasted it. *I* couldn't hide myself away from the world like he did, even if I wanted to.

I don't want to start a pity party here, but I grew up in one of the worst environments imaginable.

When I was a kid, I thought my family was normal: two ordinary parents and their son. My dad was reserved, but my mom always liked to dress up and spoke like a teenager. She embarrassed me a lot. Still, I loved my parents, and I thought they loved me, even if they messed up sometimes.

One day, my dad disappeared without warning, leaving only his debt behind. Even now, I didn't know where he went or what he was doing. My mom got her old nightlife job back to repay the debt and keep up with her lifestyle. It was only later that I learned my dad used to be a regular customer of hers. I was in high school at the time, but the only way we could afford to keep living was for me to drop out and get a job. The leftover part of my salary went to paying off Dad's debt. I was stupidly serious back then and fully believed it was my responsibility as my father's son to pay it back.

What I really wanted to do was to stay in high school and forget about the debt. I didn't want to work.

I'd worked so hard to pass the exam to get into my high school, and I only just made it. I'll never forget how crushing it was to tell them I was dropping out.

Can you see now why Yoshio seemed so spoiled to me?

I wasn't going to hate him for it, though. Where and how we grew up was out of our control. It wasn't fair to blame him.

I reminded myself over and over that he didn't do anything wrong, even if he turned his back on a future I could never have.

I was jealous, but I didn't want to hate him for something that wasn't his choice.

Besides, I had something else to live for now. My days were filled with fun, thanks to this great game—a game only I had access to. All I needed was *The Path of Destruction*. Nothing else mattered. It was the only thing that guaranteed I would be able to smile again tomorrow.

I'd been talking to Yoshio a lot; he was a great guy. He treated me with the same respect even after he learned I was a high-school dropout. I expected at least a hint of scorn from then on, but there was nothing. Unlike the rest of society—and my high-school friends—Yoshio didn't seem to place much importance on academic achievement. Since I dropped out, my old classmates acted like they were superior. When I saw them in the street, they'd pretend to ignore me before sniggering audibly as I passed them by.

I dyed my hair and got piercings to intimidate them when they saw me. We weren't going to get along ever again. I wanted the rejection to come from me, not them.

But Yoshio still treated me politely and never held his college degree over my head. More than that, whenever we were on break or in the van together, he kept on talking to me about games, just like before. Maybe I could get on with him despite our different backgrounds. Maybe he'd finally be the friend I could be myself around.

The moment I got my hopes up, I saw it.

We were in the van together, and I happened to glance at the screen of his phone. The game he was playing looked familiar.

The super-realistic graphics far too gorgeous for a video game, the characters who moved as naturally as real human beings... If that was all, I could've written it off as a different, but similar, game. But there was more.

The character names I spotted on that screen. Chem. Gams. Murus. I recognized them. They were the names left in the backlog after my camp was destroyed.

I caught on immediately. The game I was hooked on and the one Yoshio loved playing were one and the same. In the game world, he was my enemy.

Shocked was an understatement. I'd thought this guy could be my friend. Then I found out he was my enemy in the game I loved so much. He destroyed the camp I'd worked so hard for.

The more I spoke to him, the more confident I became in my suspicions. Yoshio was playing against me. I had no doubts.

He must have realized it himself by now.

I was over the moon when I snatched victory over the elven village and made all that money, but then two of my territories were destroyed, leaving me with just one. Yoshio was responsible for the destruction of one of those camps. After everything I taught him at work, *this* was how he repaid me? After telling him about my family, he still sat there grinning at his phone.

He was no different from my classmates. He was laughing at me from the shadows just like them.

Why did suffering have to come for me at every damn turn? Why did he have a perfect family who supported him, while I had no one?

My dad was gone, and Mom got herself a new man while leaving me to pay off Dad's debt. It wasn't fair!

I hated Yoshio more and more each day, and soon I couldn't even bear to look at him. I knew that he was only a small part of my problems and that I was taking everything out on him. I *knew* that, but what else was I supposed to do? While I was slaving away through no fault of my own, Yoshio was lounging around doing nothing, and I hated him for it.

Wait, wait. He's done nothing wrong, remember?

The internal fight raged on for days. My hate battled against my sense of fairness, my feelings against my conscience.

At this rate, I was going to do something stupid.

Calm down. Be rational.

There was no point stewing about it for days on end. I should just talk to him. He was a good guy. He'd be sympathetic if I told him everything. He might even let me destroy his village to help me out. If not, we could just fight fair in the game itself.

I decided that was what I'd do. I didn't want to be depressed during New Year's, either. I was just about to leave my apartment when the doorbell rang. I opened the door to find a well-dressed man standing there. I didn't recognize him, and he was at complete odds with this rundown apartment block.

"Who are you?"

"Hey. Don't worry. I'm just like you—I play *Path of Destruction*," the man explained, flicking his long bangs out of his eyes.

He plays The Path of Destruction?

I stood there, nonplussed.

"Okay...but what do you want? I was just heading out."

"I know. You're going after one of the Major Gods, right?"

How did he know? I didn't tell anyone!

"Don't look at me like that. We're both Corrupted Gods, right? We're on the same side. Just chill for a second."

The more he tried to reassure me, the more suspicious I got. Why should I trust him just because we played the same game?

"Leave, or I'm callin' the cops."

"Oh, scary! Trust me, you'll want to hear me out. I know how you can win this month's Day of Corruption, okay?"

The door was already half-closed, but I didn't push it any further.

What did he just say?

"If you let me in, I'll tell you all about it."

I felt his hand on my shoulder. When I looked up at his face, my vision blurred, and my head started spinning.

"Hey, you okay? Come on, sit. I'll tell you what I got." The man smiled.

I let him lead me back inside.

THE NPCs IN THIS VILLAGE SIM GAME MUST BE REAL! ↵

chapter 02

The Endangered Village, People, and Me

"**Y**AMAMOTO-SAN...there's no way that's you, right?" I asked the man in black, who'd just waltzed into my house, shoes and all.

Please say no...

His height, his build, the way he walked. Exactly like Yamamoto-san.

"Damn. You got me," replied the familiar voice.

The man—Yamamoto-san—pulled off his balaclava.

Ugh. Just once I'd like to be wrong.

"What are you doing here? Could you put down that crowbar? Do that, and we can just write this off as a prank."

Yamamoto-san ignored me and slowly approached. He'd seemed down lately, but now he was smiling. It wasn't a nice smile.

His eyes were bloodshot, and his mouth curled with malice. Something inside him had snapped, and it made me tremble.

"You've worked it all out, haven't you? You know what game I'm playing. You know what I'm thinking."

I stepped back from him slowly, the gears in my mind whirring.

There's only one reason he'd be here.

"You're trying to interfere with the game, right?"

"Yup. When I saw you playing on your smartphone the other day, I spotted the same names from the backlog of my own game."

"The backlog from when that one-eyed red goblin was defeated, right?"

"Exactly. I guess your college degree isn't just for show, huh?"

Was that supposed to be a compliment? Difficult to accept when he had that crowbar in his hand. I remembered Gams and the others speaking to each other back then, and I was sure they used their names. That must have been logged in Yamamoto-san's version of the game, too. If so, playing dumb here wouldn't work.

"Do what I say, and I won't do anything dangerous. You just gotta wait here till the final attack is over."

"You know this is a crime, right? You need to leave!"

"Okay, so if I told you to quit the game and surrender your village to me, you'd do it?"

"I can't."

Running was impossible—Yamamoto-san was blocking my way to the door.

What about the window?

No. My phone and PC were on the second floor. If I saved myself, Yamamoto-san could destroy them both and I'd have no way to protect my village anymore.

"I won't do anything if you don't. We can just pretend I got drunk and came to your house, and then we had a fight. I just picked up this crowbar from the toolbox on your porch, so it's not like there'd be any evidence."

Why didn't you put that away, Dad?

"No one would believe that."

"It'll be your word against mine. Who are they gonna believe? Me, or the guy who hasn't left his house in years?"

I had no answer.

As someone who contributed nothing in ten years, I was on society's lowest rung. Even if Yamamoto-san was a high school dropout, he'd worked diligently since then. He was way more sociable than me, and he had a proven track record of hard work.

It was obvious which of us society would see as more trustworthy.

"Hey, I don't wanna hurt you, y'know. I don't wanna be a criminal. So do me a favor, and just wait this out. You'll lose your game, but I'll split the money with you, if you want. It'll be a win-win."

If I did nothing, I'd come out of this richer and unharmed. I even got *The Village of Fate* for free. And even if my villagers died, even if I never saw them again, it was just a video game, right?

"Can I ask you something, Yamamoto-san?"

"What?"

"Didn't you feel bad when you attacked those villages? When you watched those highly-realistic characters getting killed?"

There was no ulterior motive behind my question. I just wanted to know. With the game's graphics, watching those people dying would be just like seeing it on the news. Some of them would have begged for their lives, elderly people and young children. What did Yamamoto-san feel—if anything—as he watched it play out?

"The hell? The graphics are realistic, yeah, but it's still a video game. Besides, even if they were real people, it's not like I know them. Does *your* heart hurt every time you watch the news and see people getting blown up in some war-torn country? Does it make *you* cry?"

That's how he sees this, huh?

"Not really...not just from watching the news. But the NPCs in this game...they *must* be real! You'd think so too if you saw how hard they worked, day after day. They work harder than I ever did in these last ten years. I feel like I *do* know them." I held my ground and stared intently at Yamamoto-san.

I was putting my life in danger for the sake of some video game characters, and that sounded stupid, but I *owed* them this life. They saved me when I was at my lowest! I couldn't just sell them out.

"Are you stupid? You know, I thought we could be friends. It's a shame this is what you're really like."

"Please think about what you're doing, Yamamoto-san."

"Do you have any idea what I've been through? Just because I was born into a crappy family, I had to drop out of high school and work through all my teens and twenties to pay back a debt that wasn't mine. Now look at *you*! You've lived here without needing to lift a finger for years! You don't even know the value of money!"

Yamamoto-san's eyes were dark with rage. "Ten years of doing nothing! Do you know how much it must've cost your family to support you for just one of those years? Do you know how much of your family's hard-earned money you've sat around wasting?"

I couldn't answer him.

I always thought I was cursed. That it was society's fault. That it didn't matter because it wasn't like I was getting in anyone's way. Those were the excuses I clung to these past ten years.

"This is my one chance to make something of myself. I don't have the qualifications or skills to do anything else. There's no point saying shit like 'things will get better,' either. They won't. As far as society's concerned, if you didn't go to college and get a job straight out of it, you've missed the boat!"

Again, I had no answer.

I was lucky to be born where I was, yet I did nothing to show any gratitude. I let the chance to lead a proper life slip away from me. Any words I said would be empty and useless. My words were powerless.

"Why are you crying? *I'm* the one who should be crying!"

I'm crying?

Was I crying out of sympathy for him or at my own pathetic life? I couldn't work it out, but I couldn't stop the tears, either.

"Yamamoto-san...your life is worth ten of mine."

"What? Is that supposed to be sarcasm?"

"No. I wasted ten whole years of my life, not realizing how lucky I was. All I needed was a tiny bit of courage to change things, but I was too wrapped up in self-pity to gather that courage."

I wish I'd realized sooner. I wish I'd *done* something sooner. What would my life be like now if I had? Maybe I could've shown Seika a happy life. Maybe I could've helped my family with their troubles. Instead, I was nothing but a burden.

"I don't need your pity. But if you wanna do something for me now, then just shut up and watch. It's time for the Day of Corruption's final attack." Yamamoto thrust his phone in front of my face.

"The Day of Corruption: Final Wave!" flashed in red letters on the screen.

"This is my all-out attack! The attack I've poured all my money into! If this ain't enough to destroy your village, then it's game over for me. So let me have it."

There were dozens...no, *hundreds* of monsters on the screen swarming towards my village.

My villagers can't fight that many!

Several of the enemies were powerful-looking creatures I'd never even seen before. At this rate, my village was doomed. Even if I could get the golem out, victory was uncertain.

Gams, Chem, Carol, Rodice, Lyra, Murus, Kan, Lan...were they all going to die?

What do I do?! How can I save them?

My thoughts were scattered, my panic only increasing.

The front door clicked open.

"Have you got a friend around? I heard shouting."

Seika walked into the living room. I stared at her.

She couldn't have picked a worse time!

"Wh-who are you? A burglar?"

"Shut up!" Yamamoto turned and raised the bar above his head.

My mind went blank as the blood started to boil in my veins. Before I knew it, I was moving. I vaulted over the couch and barreled into Yamamoto. He was short, and I bowled him over, the two of us flying into the wall. If I could get ahold of the crowbar and pin him down, I could stop him from doing anything else. The next moment I felt a sharp pain in my back. Someone screamed.

Did he get me in the back with the crowbar?

"I told you just to do what I said! This is your own fault! Your fault for making fun of me, just 'cause I'm poor!"

He struck my back again and again. Even when the pain was unbearable, he hit me again, the metal bar smashing over and over into that same spot. It hurt so bad I couldn't even scream. The hot blood that burned in me before had gone as cold as ice.

I knew he must have broken some bones, and I also knew now that the shows I watched where characters kept fighting despite their injuries were bullshit. I could hardly keep my mind together.

Why did I try to save Seika if it was going to end in so much pain? Did I think I was a hero? I couldn't even feel the hands gripping onto Yamamoto anymore—every sensation in my body was overrun with pain. I wanted...a way out. I wanted to die.

But I couldn't let go of him. If I let go, he'd turn on Seika. I promised myself I wouldn't feel that regret for the rest of my life.

"Run...Sei...ka... Run!"

"I-I can't!" Seika sobbed.

"Don't... Don't make me regret this! Seika! *Run!*" I screamed at her with the last of my strength.

"I'll go get help!" she gasped, tear-stricken.

She ran for the open front door.

"You're not going anywhere!" Yamamoto's face twisted with monstrous rage as he raised the crowbar above his head to throw.

Seika looked over her shoulder, her face growing pale with horror.

I gotta do something! But the pain paralyzed me. I pleaded with my body. *Come on! Move!*

Somehow pushing through the pain, I reached out and only just managed to get my hands around Yamamoto's wrist. Fearing the worst, I squeezed my eyes shut, but neither a fresh rush of pain, nor Seika's scream, ever came.

"Let go! You—wait! My hands! What's happenin' to my hands?!"

I slowly opened my eyes. Yamamoto was staring at his arm in shock.

"I-I can't move my arm! What's goin' on?! What's happening?!" Yamamoto cradled his right arm, which was slowly stiffening and turning stone gray. "W-wait! Did *you* do this?!"

Yamamoto wasn't scowling at me. I followed his gaze. He was glaring at Destiny.

When did you get here?!

It walked up to us slowly.

"Stay back, you monster! What the fuck is that thing?! Keep it away from—" Yamamoto was interrupted by a bout of violent coughing.

Destiny perched itself on his stiffened arm, opened its mouth, and let out a puff of purple smoke right in his face. Yamamoto fell to the floor, tears and snot streaming down.

"What...what...that lizard..." Seika sank down to the floor, confusion and fear in her eyes as she repeated the same words over and over.

Destiny trotted up to her and licked her face. Seika screeched and fainted.

Being licked in the face by a creature that terrified her—right after everything she'd just witnessed—must have been too much for her. I wanted to thank Destiny, but I was still in too much agony to speak. Destiny hopped up on the table and stuck its hand into my wallet before pulling something out.

That's Murus's herbal mix!

Destiny pulled out the stopper with its teeth and brought the tube to my mouth. It waited, apparently wanting me to drink it. I forced my mouth open, and Destiny poured the contents of the tube inside. I swallowed, and the pain disappeared at once.

"And...I can talk again!"

I tried moving my limbs. They moved freely, as though nothing had happened. I pulled up my top and touched my back where the crowbar hit me. I wasn't even bruised. I repressed the urge to start dancing in praise of that incredible medicine.

What happened to the village?!

I was just about to race upstairs when I found a phone thrust in front of my face. Destiny must have picked it up from my room for me. I looked at the screen.

The fence was burning, and my villagers were covered in blood.

THE NPCs IN THIS VILLAGE SIM GAME MUST BE REAL! ↵

Epilogue

WHILE I WAS FIGHTING Yamamoto, my village was on the verge of destruction. The fence around the cave was partially uprooted in some areas and totally burned down in others. A huge chunk had been torn out of the planks protecting the cave entrance, exposing the interior to the outside air. The door to the innermost room—Kan and Lan's old room—was open, with Rodice's family inside, huddled together and trembling. Kan and Lan's fur was matted with blood as they held each other up, staggering into the room. Murus was holding a short sword in one hand, her other arm twisted at an impossible angle. Gams's armor was in tatters, and the blood from his wounds had dried sticky on his skin, but he was still fighting. Chem was behind him, desperately performing as many healing spells as she could through gritted teeth, her eyes filled with tears.

There were still dozens of monsters in front of them.

"I'm so sorry, guys! I'm coming!"

I grabbed the phone from Destiny and activated the miracle to summon the golem...but nothing happened.

"What?! Why isn't it working?!"

I tapped the button again and again, but it made no difference. Gams and Murus were slowly being forced back to the room where Rodice's family and the pandas were sheltering. Gams, Murus, and Chem caught each other's eyes before they too dove into that room and slammed the door behind them. Monsters clawed and banged. That room was the emergency shelter, and the door was reinforced, but at this rate, it would only be a few minutes before the monsters broke through. Kan and Lan looked like they had already given up. They were huddled up in a corner, their backs to the door.

"Why won't the golem activate?! I have enough FP!" I kept pressing the button desperately, but nothing changed.

"This might be it," Rodice murmured, a sad smile on his face.

"Don't say that!" I cried.

"Yes...I'm afraid it might be. Thank you, everyone. You protected me and my helpless family." Lyra bowed her head, and her husband followed suit.

Carol was asleep, and even now she wasn't waking up.

"Thanks to Murus's sleeping herbs, our daughter can go peacefully," Rodice said, looking at Carol.

"I don't think we can expect any miracles, since the Lord's statue was broken. We shall be with you soon, Lord." Chem clutched a small, finger-shaped piece of wood in her hand.

My statue was destroyed? That's why I can't activate the golem... but I can't give up yet! There's gotta be some other miracle I can use!

"Sorry, everyone. I wasn't strong enough. I wasn't strong enough to protect you!" Gams's fists trembled as a drop of blood seeped out through his gritted teeth.

"I'm going to lose my home and my friends all over again. This time, I'm going to lose my life, too." Murus slammed the ground with the bow she clutched in her fist.

Stop it! Stop! It's not over yet! There's gotta be some way I can save you!

Should I write them a prophecy telling them not to give up? How the hell was that supposed to help? There had to be some way to turn this situation around!

Think! Think! Think, think, think, think…

"I never thought we'd have to use this, but we can't die for nothing." Gams picked up the wooden box that lay in the opposite corner from Kan and Lan's huddling spot.

The explosives designed to blow up bedrock. Was he going to blow the cave up with them still in it?

"There is a chance one of us could still be saved, even if we use this," Chem said. "But only one of us."

I gasped along with the other villagers. Kan and Lan turned around.

"Well, I'm not sure if 'saved' is the correct word, but at the very least, they won't die. Who should we pick?"

The villagers glanced at each other and then all looked at the same person.

"I thought so. Lord, please take good care of her. Please forgive us for throwing away your blessing of life like this."

Chem's smile was the last thing I saw before the screen went black.

"No! Why's the screen gone black? This is a joke, right? It can't end like this!" I collapsed to the floor, no longer able to support my own weight.

The screen stayed black. My mind went blank. I wanted it to stay that way. I didn't want to move.

There was a strange vibrating sound. I looked at my phone, but that wasn't what was making the noise. I moved my lifeless eyes around the room and realized the sound was coming from Yamamoto's phone. I glanced at the red letters on the screen.

"Game over. You are no longer eligible to play."

My villagers' bomb must have wiped out his monsters.

I only resented Yamamoto a little bit for the deaths of my villagers, but even that resentment was fading now. There was more text on the screen.

"All your memories pertaining to the game will now be wiped."

"Huh?"

That wasn't in the contract! I didn't know we'd forget everything if we got a game over. In fact, if they *did* put that in the contract, I wouldn't have believed them at first. Now, things were different.

I'd seen Destiny's power firsthand. I'd experienced the healing effects of Murus's herbs. After that, I could believe anything.

If Yamamoto lost his memories of the game, did that mean he'd forget everything that happened here tonight?

I did despise him for what he did to my villagers, but after hearing everything he had to say, I couldn't bring myself to hate him completely. It was a shallower emotion than that. This game sent Yamamoto...san over the edge. If his memories disappeared, he should go back to his usual cheerful self, right? I wanted to scream at him for what he did, but there would be no point if he didn't know what I was talking about. Should I even hand him over to the police? I mean, he *did* commit a crime. With my body totally healed, though, there was no evidence of violence.

If he got sent to prison without any memory of what he'd done, he'd definitely hold a grudge. How many years would he get? Probably not that many. What would happen when he got out? He could beat me up all he wanted, that wouldn't be an issue. I was more concerned that it might cause yet more trouble for my family.

Through all this, I kept thinking about how every time I messed up at work, or got in Yamamoto-san's way, he'd tell me not to worry about it. He'd just tell me to fix it, and then he'd come with me to get chewed out by the boss later.

Gathering the last pieces of my rational mind, I suppressed my waning rage and let out a deep sigh. I looked over at Yamamoto-san's unconscious body, and I could swear I saw a faint black mist escaping from him and vanishing into the air. I rubbed my eyes, but when I looked again, I couldn't see anything like that. His arm no longer looked stiff, and his breathing was back to normal.

"Was that... I mean, you did that, right? And then you fixed him?" I asked Destiny, though I already knew the answer.

Destiny gave a small nod.

This lizard of mine had impossible powers. I should probably be terrified, but I wasn't. Destiny was family, and it saved me.

"Thanks, Destiny." I stroked its head gently. It narrowed its eyes at me. "Guess I'll have to tidy everything up now."

I took Seika, who was still unconscious, and laid her on a futon in the next room. Then I put Yamamoto-san on the couch. I didn't want to do anything right now, but I needed some way to distract myself. I quickly wiped at my eyes and headed into the kitchen. I took out two of Dad's beers, emptied them into the sink, and placed the empty cans on the table in the living room. I put a couple of empty plates and open snack packets next to them.

How much would Yamamoto-san remember? Perhaps I should wait and see before deciding what to do.

"Destiny, could you hide? I'm counting on you to help if I end up in danger again, though, okay?" I said, before turning my attention to Yamamoto-san and shaking his shoulder. "Yamamoto-san, wake up. It's pretty late."

Yamamoto-san blinked open his eyes in confusion. "H-Huh? Where am I? Yoshio? What are you doin' here?"

"Are you still drunk? You got drunk and came over, then drank some more, and we had a kinda party, but you fell asleep. You don't remember?"

"I don't... My head feels real woozy. I feel like I met someone this afternoon, and then..."

If he was acting, he deserved an Oscar. It looked to me like he really had forgotten. Besides, if he could act that well, he could've used that to trick me today instead of resorting to threats.

He had no rage left in his eyes. He looked around the room in a daze. It reminded me of people in movies waking up after an exorcism.

"You shouldn't drink so much that it affects your memory. You said you were supposed to go home before the year ticks over. Think you can make it?"

"I did? Uh...I feel like there was somethin' I was supposed to do. But I'm sorry for coming over like this." Yamamoto-san scratched his head awkwardly.

I wanted to yell at him for being so nonchalant. I wanted to punch some sense into him. Rage welled up in my chest, but all I could do was push it back down.

"Please be more careful from now on."

"Yeah. I'm really sorry for causin' you trouble. I'll get going now."

"Okay. Happy New Year."

I showed him to the door and shut it behind him. I waited for a few seconds, and then I punched the wall.

Ow...

More than the pain, more than the anger, I felt empty inside.

"It's all over, huh? Just like that. I couldn't give my villagers a good life in the end." I slumped back against the front door and slid to the floor.

I lost everything.

I looked back at my phone clutched in my hand. The screen was still black.

"I got a game over, too. Does this mean I've forgotten all about—No!"

I never saw the game over message on *my* phone, and I still had my memories of the game.

"What does it mean? Okay, calm down. Calm down and think."

When Yamamoto-san got a game over, his phone buzzed and that message in red appeared on the screen, but I didn't see anything like that on mine. It was possible I missed it in all the confusion, but I could still remember everything about the game.

"Gams, Chem, Rodice, Lyra, Carol, Murus, Kan, Lan. I can remember their names, their faces, their personalities..."

This had to mean that my village was still standing. It wasn't game over for me. Right?!

But then why was my screen still blank? I touched it, and some red letters appeared.

"*The holy book does not exist on the current map.*"

"That's 'cause it got blown up, right? But then shouldn't I have a game over?"

Things were only getting more confusing.

At that second, the doorbell rang.

"Huh?! Ow!"

I jumped at the sound, hitting my head on the doorknob above it. At this time of night, I could only imagine it was Yamamoto-san coming back for something.

I stood up and opened the door. There was a huge cardboard box on the doorstep. The sender was listed as "The Village of Fate."

"Huh?"

My thoughts began to race as everything became more nonsensical. I told my villagers they didn't need to send me anything on the Day of Corruption so we could focus on overcoming it. I didn't see my villagers put anything on the altar all day, so it didn't make sense for a parcel to show up at my door.

"It says it's from the game, though."

It was bigger than any other cardboard box they'd sent me. The logs were large, of course, but they didn't come in a box. If I wanted to know what this was, my only choice was to open it. I leaned down to pick it up and take it inside, but it was heavier than it looked, so I dragged it onto the porch instead. I took a deep breath and opened it.

Inside was a girl clutching a familiar book to her chest. She had blonde, wavy hair and a cherubic face. Though she was usually running around with a huge smile, right now she was sleeping peacefully.

"Carol?!"

The Village of Fate was supposed to be over, but it looked like its story was going to continue. Whether this was reality or just a hallucination, I wasn't sure. The game and reality collided, and now a new story was ready to start.

What was waiting for me when this girl finally woke up? Even the God of Fate himself couldn't say.

THE NPCs IN THIS VILLAGE SIM GAME MUST BE REAL! ↵

Commentary of
THIS WORLD

This world is perilous, but our devotion will see us through it. This book will show us the way.

01.
The Cave

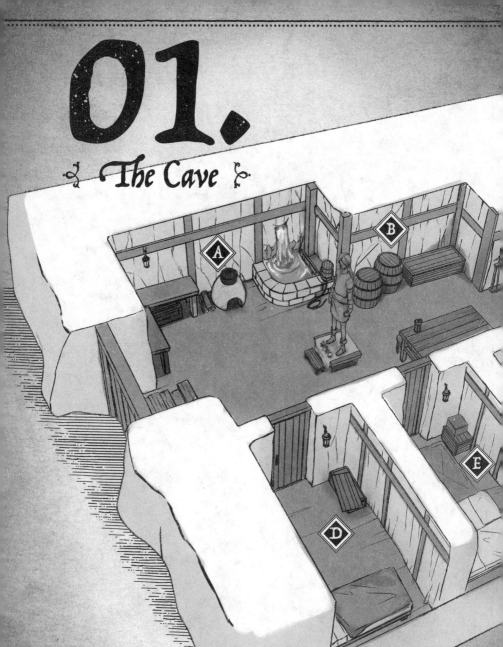

Village Floorplan

A floorplan of the cave the villagers live in. A former mine, the miners used to live and store their tools here.

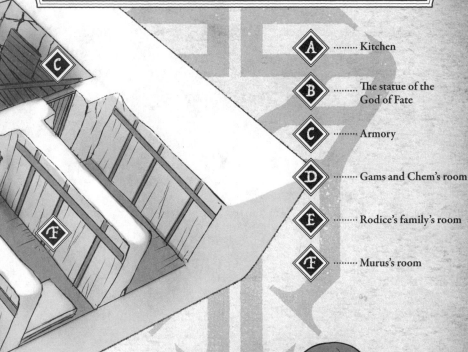

A .... Kitchen

B .... The statue of the God of Fate

C .... Armory

D .... Gams and Chem's room

E .... Rodice's family's room

F .... Murus's room

Murus told us about this cave, and we decided to move here! We've got a kitchen, and everyone has a room! I'm lucky enough to share with my brother... hee hee!

CHEM'S VOICE

02.

⚘ Beastfolk ⚘

Species: BEARCAT

These two lived with the dwarves and humans who used to call the cave home. They are a couple and generally keep to themselves. They might look cute, but they are very skilled with their hands. Carpenters by trade, they are also proficient with explosives and spears. Lan is the male and has the thicker fur of the two (left). Kan is the female and has thinner fur (right).

Lan & Kan

Destiny

03.

⚘ Familiar ⚘

Species: BASILISK

A familiar that hatched from an egg Yoshio got from the egg gacha. Carol placed the egg innocently on the altar, sending it to Yoshio's house. It looks like a lizard but is actually a basilisk. It will eat anything other than bugs but likes the meat and fruit sent from the Village of Fate best. It's a popular member of Yoshio's family and escapes from its tank on a near-daily basis. An intelligent creature, it likes to watch over Yoshio's villagers with him.

Afterword

THANK YOU SO MUCH for buying volume two. What did you think? This story was also posted on *Let's Be Novelists*, but I made a lot of improvements and corrections for the published version, just like with volume one. More than a third of this book is new material, so I think even fans of the web-novel will find it enjoyable to read. One of the major changes is that the published version has more scenes from other characters' perspective—both in the game and in the real-life setting. I also added the episode about Yoshio asking the villagers for advice.

I also want to talk about the new characters in volume two. First, there's the introduction of Yoshio's childhood friend, who he reunites with after cutting off contact. I hope you'll look forward to seeing how Yoshio deals with it, even though he's conflicted. With the help of his villagers, Yoshio works towards repairing their relationship.

There's also Lan and Kan, who are a beastfolk couple that joins the Village of Fate. They're just so cute! They're bipedal red pandas—so of course they're adorable. The illustrations

Namako-sensei drew for them make them look even cuter. I hope you'll look at them again and again and smile as much as I did!

Now, there's one more character that can't go unmentioned. I've heard that some readers think it's the series' main heroine. I'm talking about Destiny, the golden lizard.

To be honest, I didn't really like reptiles, but after I began doing research, I started thinking they were cute. Destiny's best features are its slightly rounded belly and big, round eyes. Not only is it cute, but it's become Yoshio's trusted partner. It will be sticking with him for a long time, so look forward to seeing more of it in the story!

That's about it for characters, so I'd like to move on to talking about the plot.

Were you surprised where Sayuki's incident led? How about the plot twist near the epilogue? Then there's the incident in the past that was part of why Yoshio became a NEET. This volume covers how he deals with all those things.

Then there's the last scene right at the end. I know there are people who read the afterword before the story itself, so I can't go into much detail, but this final scene divided my audience when I posted it online. I could have changed it for the published version, but I didn't want to. This series was always meant to be split into three parts. If I changed it now, it would derail the rest of the series.

In the published version, part one became volume one. Part two became volume two, and so part three will likely be wrapped up in volume three. If you didn't like the ending of this volume,

I would urge you to see what happens in volume three. I'm confident you'll change your mind about it when you do. But then again, if this volume doesn't sell, there might not be a third, so please tell all your friends about it!

Oh, wait! There was one more important thing I wanted to say. In case you didn't already know, the manga version of *The NPCs in the Village Sim Game Must Be Real* is being published in *Young Ace UP* right now. Kazuhiko Morita-sensei is doing a great job at making my story several times more charming than I could hope to make it by myself. Don't miss it!

Now I'd like to say my thank-yous.

First, I want to thank my illustrator, Namako-sensei. It must've been tough drawing all the non-human characters that showed up in volume two, but you drew Lan, Kan, and Destiny perfectly! Your drawings of them are too adorable! You drew Seika so well, too. She's totally my type!

I'd also like to thank Kazuhiko Morita-sensei, who's in charge of the manga version. Thank you so much for your amazing work on it! I'm always so excited for the next installment that I get really nervous the day before.

To my designers, proofreaders, the printers, and my editor, N-sama, thank you for your support once again. To everyone who was involved in the publication of this volume, I'm afraid I can't do anything more than thank you in the afterword, but it was all because of you that I managed to put out the best book possible. Finally, thank you so much to everyone who bought a copy of this book and everyone who bought volume one.

It's thanks to every one of you that volume two was published. I hope you'll keep supporting me in the future.

—HIRUKUMA

To be continued...